Praise for

"Literature about literature, writi (?), words independent of their m impossibility of communication, but risk and generosity, a bet on the void, failure foretold, but literature, in short. A pleasure but more difficult than ever. Pilgrim readers, you've been advised."—Rafael Conte

"[Coll's literature] seems to have emerged from the same source that produced James Joyce's Finnegans Wake and the writing of Samuel Beckett and Guillermo Cabrera Infante, but which moves from a stance of detachment and skepticism regarding the literature's power toward the staggering loneliness of the artist, who must carry out his task blindly, with no one with whom to converse."—Patricio Pron

"Aliocha Coll will never die ... because death comes when nobody remembers you, and Aliocha will be remembered for centuries."
—Carmen Balcells

"I asked [Coll] why he didn't try to do something less avant-garde. He truly had a lot of literary talent and could have done anything. One must admit that his texts were very hermetic. It was unlikely that an editor would risk publishing something that a more conventional reader wouldn't understand."—Javier Marías

ATTILA

Aliocha Coll

Prologue by Javier Serena

Translated from Spanish by Katie Whittemore

OPEN LETTER
LITERARY TRANSLATIONS FROM THE UNIVERSITY OF ROCHESTER

Originally published in Spanish as *Atila* by Destino, 1991

Copyright © Aliocha Coll, 1991 and Heirs of Aliocha Coll

Translation copyright © Katie Whittemore, 2025

First edition, 2025

All rights reserved

Library of Congress Control Number: 2024952355

ISBN (pb): 978-1-960385-37-6| ISBN (ebook): 978-1-960385-38-3

This project is made possible by the New York State Council on the Arts with the support of the Office of the Governor and the New York State Legislature.

Cover design by Daniel Benneworth-Gray

Published by Open Letter at the University of Rochester

Morey Hall 303, Rochester NY, 14627

www.openletterbooks.org

Printed on acid-free paper.

ATTILA

TABLE OF CONTENTS

ON TRANSLATING COLL

One must always write as if one could not write.

Aliocha Coll, *Attila*

Publishing Atila *is an experimental gamble offering little commercial guarantee.*

Andreu Teixidor, director of the publisher Destino, in 1991

*

In 2019, over basketball and beer, Chad W. Post of Open Letter Books and I discuss the potential of publishing two of young Spanish writer Javier Serena's novels, both of which are dedicated to real literary figures and plumb the intense personal and social dynamics surrounding creative endeavors. One is a fictionalized account of a writer inspired by (fan favorite) Roberto Bolaño, and the other an homage to the final years of a solitary, uncompromising character based on a certain ... Aliocha Coll?

A cursory Google search yields intriguing information. This Coll was a friend of Javier Marías, and characters based on him appear in several of Marías's works; he was Carmen Balcells's only unsuccessful client; he lived a kind of ascetic life in Paris; he is forgotten, impossible, cursed, brilliant, a cult writer.

Atila (*Attila* in English, which is how I'll refer to it from here on out), his final book, was published by Destino in 1991 and, in 2019, is out of print (though it will be later be republished by Galaxia Gutenberg in 2023). It is the direct inspiration for Javier Serena's novel by the same name.

The Carmen Balcells Agency sends us a PDF of a scanned copy of Destino's 1991 edition of *Attila*, which is all they have. The two-book translation project becomes a triptych: two Serenas, and a Coll.

Between that moment and this one, a dozen translation projects intervene. "The Attilas" are delayed. And delayed again. But in a twist, the Attilas will now be published when I'm 42, Coll's age when he wrote the novel's last words and took his own life shortly after.

*

> *Aliocha Coll passed through Spanish literature like a clandestine meteor, like a blind star, like a black hole.*
>
> Rafael Conte, 1991 review of *Attila* in *ABC*

*

When I start to write about Coll's biographical details, I find myself recalling sketches and snippets from Serena's *Attila*, which—as he recently confirmed—contains many invented details. Serena, it seems, is much more interested in rescuing the spirit of Aliocha than writing a biography (though perhaps that is to come) and thus didn't hold back on the fictionalization. Yet having spent time in both men's worlds, Serena's Alioscha becomes as real to me as Aliocha (who is actually another Javier; Aliocha was a pseudonym, a nod to his mother, who read *The Brothers Karamazov* while pregnant). I have to remind myself that the real Coll did not, in fact, have a tempestuous and violent relationship with his father as portrayed in Serena's novel.

*

Aliocha Coll was born Javier Coll Mata on May 6, 1948, in Madrid. Though born in the Spanish capital, he grew up in Barcelona, where his family was from, and where he began his studies in Medicine. He married the French-Chinese painter Lysiane Luong, from whom he later separated. I read that they might have conceived a baby, who did not survive. I don't know if this is true. He translated Christopher Marlowe beautifully. When Coll ran short on money from his family income, he practiced medicine on weekends. On November 15, 1990, in Paris, he died by suicide.

*

Published Works

Vitam venturi saeculi (1982)

Títeres, a children's play written with Lysiane Luong (1984)

Translation of work by Christopher Marlowe (1984)

Atila (1991, posthumous)

El hilo de seda (1992, posthumous)

Imaginarias, a poetry collection (1999, posthumous)

*

In a spring 2023 session, my medium, K, refers to a translation I'm reluctant to start. "I don't know if this will make sense to you, but it feels . . . chaotic . . . like, really challenging. You're just going to have to interpret it. You're free to do that." On the way to my appointment, I'd had a bit of a heated phone exchange with Chad about *Attila*. I'm dragging my feet. I want to bring other people in to help. Chad is frustrated that the excitement we had for the project seems to have dissipated on my end. I grumble. *Just wait, you'll see.* K asks if I recognize the work she's describing. Has the author passed? His energy is odd, she can't quite grasp what it is exactly, but he's unusual. And grateful, apparently. K tells me he offers to "be with me" and help when I translate. She says I can call him in for short periods when I'm working, but to make sure to "close it down," when I'm done. You don't really want to hang around in that energy, she advises. *Hm, okay.*

I don't light any candles or draw a circle with salt or anything like that. I don't invoke Aliocha in any ritual capacity. I do, however, find myself open to the possibility that some part of him is present with me in this process.

*

By all accounts, Coll was a good person. Valued highly by those who knew him. Considerate. Educated. Old-fashioned in his mannerisms. Surely eccentric. Extraordinarily well-read for sure. A genius? Perhaps.

*

When the time came for us to meet, in Barcelona, I remember expecting to find an individual looking wild or eccentric or iconoclastic; instead, a there appeared a young man, impeccably dressed, dapper, even, with excellent manners, an old-fashioned face that seemed to have come out of the 1930s, and with literary, musical, artistic, and philosophical knowledge that I would have liked to have myself. Contrary to what I'd naively assumed after reading his books, he wasn't at all contemptuous of the past; on the contrary, he felt so connected to it that it was for this very reason, he explained, that he chose to write the way he did. "Mondrian hasn't yet reached literature," he said.

Javier Marías in his obituary for Coll

*

He was handsome, I think, or at least he seems so to me, judging from the few photographs I've seen of him online. I read that someone once joked that there was something of Arnold Schwarzenegger about him, just in the face, and if I let my eyes unfocus, I think maybe I can see it. But it's the literary heroicism of his figure that does it for me—the accursed poet, the damaged, gallant lover, a dapperly-dressed man out of time, wholly committed to his literary values, living in self-imposed precarity—in Paris of all places—and writing for what Javier Serena assures me was an audience of one: Coll himself. It's hard *not* to romanticize him. I imagine him scribbling away, struggling—did he hear voices, did he dream premonitory dreams?—refusing to compromise on his art, making himself sick on literature. Ah yes, that's a man for me! Younger Katie would have wanted to mother him, keep his house, make his meals, love him back from the edge. But ho! What reactionary yearnings are these? What mythic projections?

*

"My life will be meaningless when Atila is finished," he'd said more than once. [. . .] Three days prior to his death, Carmen Balcells received the manuscript. It was his literary testament.

Xavier Moret in *El País*, November 1991

*

I learn to experience *Attila* without needing to grasp, hold, dominate, or explain it. I quickly realize that what I normally do as a translator isn't going to work. In the first place, I barely understand what I'm reading. The first pages of the book are a genre-busting blend of drama and prose and poetry, addressing and invoking mythological and historical figures, like Laocoön, with whom I'm only glancingly familiar, and others I've never heard of at all. And though I sense that what I'm reading is not stream of consciousness, but rather words arranged on the page with care, the metaphors and images are so abstract and the references so obscure and the pace so galloping that I doubt myself. And what are these geometry terms? MATH?! Shit. I start to sweat.

*

As I work, ChatGPT is spawning a million think pieces and X posts and roundtables. Hand-wringing and swearing-off abound. I agree, in large part, with these sentiments, but I think it's a tool that can have its place. It becomes a kind of research assistant, helping me sort through the huge number of references. I do feel a bit guilty, imagining how Aliocha would view my recurring to AI when he held so much in his brain. Sometimes the tool helps. Other times, it is politely, deferentially useless.

> is sigilegio a word in spanish?

No, **"sigilegio"** is not a standard word in Spanish. It might be a typo, a rare or archaic term, or a neologism (a newly coined word) not widely recognized in dictionaries.

If you meant something like **"sigil"** (related to symbols or mystical signs), the term could be **"sigilo"** (meaning stealth or secrecy), or **"sigil"** in the context of magical or occult practices. It could also possibly relate to **"siglo"** (century) if it was a typo.

Could you clarify the context where you encountered the word? This might help in identifying the intended meaning.

◁» ⬠ ⚐ ♡ ↻˅

An **abscissa** is a term used in mathematics, particularly in coordinate geometry, to refer to the **x-coordinate** of a point in a two-dimensional Cartesian coordinate system. In a coordinate pair (x, y), the **abscissa** is the value of **x**, which represents the horizontal position of the point on the graph.

Is there a story or painting or cultural reference to an Amazon and a "lazarilla"? or a horsewoman and flower seller's guide?

‹ 3/3 ›

The combination of an "Amazon" (a mythological warrior woman) and a "lazarilla" (which could refer to a figure related to the Spanish *lazarillo*, or a servant, often depicted in literature as poor or marginalized) does not seem to have a direct, famous cultural or artistic reference in history. However, I can see how the idea of an Amazon—representing strength and independence—could be paired with the figure of a *lazarilla*, suggesting a juxtaposition between mythological power and the humbler, more grounded realities of dail ↓ e.

*

There are writers who make no concessions, which is why their books are marked by that particular vocation for secrecy. Not only is it diffi-cult to find such works, but even when you've gotten a copy, you then have to engage with writing that has few models, is outside tastes and trends, and indifferent to the reader's gratification.

Fernando Valls on Aliocha Coll

*

Translators like to think of themselves as "good readers," close readers who can reach the heart of a work and—almost alchemically—create another version of it in English. For me, this process often feels intuitive. But with Coll, my flow is constantly broken, violently so, by a sense of bewilderment and frustration. I'm forced to work very slowly, looking up more words than ever before as a long-time reader of works in Spanish. *Attila* elides and eludes. There is some relief when I reach the second part of the book, a love story, on the surface, and a meditation on history, civilization, and art, and here, yes, there are things that make narrative sense. Yet once I depart Rome with Quixote and Ipsibidimidiata, I am plunged again into a literal dark cave, then a strange forest.

*

I visit Paris while translating *Attila*. In the morning, I sit downstairs in the hotel café with my laptop and copy of the book. I plan to get an hour of work in before we start our day. My friend, a writer, joins me and I show her what I'm working on. It's kind of a nightmare, I say. A few hours later, we stand on a bridge over the Seine and watch the tourist boats motoring below. I want to connect with Aliocha. I open the channel, which feels a bit like a slackening of my physical body and a tightening of something else, the air around me maybe, and I feel heat in my arms and tingling in my hands.

*

[*Coll's literature*] *seems to have emerged from the same source that produced James Joyce's Finnegans Wake and the writing of Samuel Beckett and Guillermo Cabrera Infante, but which moves from a stance of detachment and skepticism regarding the literature's power toward the staggering loneliness of the artist, who must carry out his task blindly, with no one with whom to converse.*

Patricio Pron on *Attila*

*

I encounter beautiful images, startling turns of phrase, hints of philosophical and even metaphysical reflections, explosions and purrs. I perceive this and can appreciate it. I find satisfaction in what I do understand, in the visuals Coll's words make bloom behind my eyelids, but mostly I fear that I don't really get it. I certainly don't like it, not in the way we usually "like" books. I realize that this is the point. And I must translate it that way. My translation is going to have to be as freaking unpleasant to read as Coll's *Attila* often is. I stop fretting about what readers of my translation will think, how they might judge this text as unreadable translationese. I stop fretting about these imaginary readers and remember that Aliocha didn't have his readers in mind either. He didn't actually have readers, at least not while he lived. Our *Attila* won't have many of them either, I think. A weight lifts. I undertake a new approach. Instead of drowning at the ground level of words and sentences, I pull up. I imagine myself soaring, like a bird, over a landscape below, and the landscape is *Attila*. I also start translating very literally. In many places I don't even change the syntax, and I don't automatically look for an alternative to simple cognates. My own sanity rests on simply getting the book done. This time, that will be enough.

*

Do what you can for my work, though there's not much that can be done.

Coll, to his agent Carmen Balcells

*

An October 2024 email from Javier Serena:

> And that's why I believe that, on one hand, Coll perfectly achieves his narrative project: to create unintelligible literature (poetic, free of plot and chronology, dedicated to language, its rhythm, its musicality, a plasticity that goes beyond grammar and correctness). And at the same time, there was only one possible reader for that narrative project: himself. He succeeded in his project, but his project is a failure. And that impossibility—this hopeless negativity—is what makes Aliocha and his books so unique. "Impossible to write, impossible to stop writing," he used to say.

*

I get an idea to paint scenes, selected at random, from *Attila*.

> *Fleeces of amethyst gas, ripped from green chaparral by the western blush, pirouetted gracelessly in their ascent toward the rust, where an oscillating breath vaporized old blood clots.*

*

Javier sends me another email. A folder is attached: "Aliocha Coll Inéditos," containing unpublished work by Coll, including his essay on pain, a kind of thesis for his medical degree. *What sense has the mind made of pain, of this state of consciousness?* I read somewhere that Coll purportedly experimented with pain on his own body. The essay was written on a typewriter and afterward, someone—Aliocha, I presume—has gone through the text with a pen and manually added the accents marks. At the bottom of the page, the same hand has signed *Paris, 1982.*

*

Literature about literature, writing for writers, complimentary music (?), words independent of their meaning, experimental to the extreme, impossibility of communication, but risk and generosity, a bet on the void, failure foretold, but literature, in short. A pleasure but more difficult than ever. Pilgrim readers, you've been advised.

Rafael Conte, 1991 review of *Atila* in *ABC*

*

The night I finish the draft of my translation, I receive a gift from Coll. I dream I'm sitting in a snug in an Irish pub, seated at a small and dark wooden table. From the sky, a rock drops straight through the roof and crashes down on the table in front of me. It is the size of my palm. My first dream thought is that the stone could have killed me. I pick it up and immediately I know—the way we immediately know in dreams—that the stone is lapis lazuli. Lapis lazuli, the dream self knows. From Aliocha, the dream self hears.

PROLOGUE

Errant companion in words, in silences
and in centuries.

ALIOCHA COLL, in his dedication of
Vitam venturi saeculi to Javier Marías

Have we read Aliocha Coll properly? Will future readers, more attuned to his work's complexities, appreciate it in ways that elude us, despite our intuitive sense of its value? These are questions that inevitably arise when we engage with his work, including the posthumously published *Attila*, a novel that embodies the distinctive avant-garde style, marked by attention to rhythm and surrealist lyricism, found in his fiction. And though these characteristics have earned Coll praise, navigating his work presents serious challenges: finding coherence in the discourse, deciphering the logic in each sentence, and following a narrative thread are formidable tasks in this meticulously crafted yet enigmatic novel.

The prevailing response to Coll's work has been one of perplexity. Critics, acknowledging his talent, education, and audacious approach to literature, find themselves caught in a paradox: while they respect and recognize his rejection of literary convention, his deep exploration of tradition, and his quest for innovation, they struggle to fully embrace books that resist interpretation and communication. It's as if the very essence of his writing sought to negate itself, which perhaps reflects the author's acute awareness of the inherent inadequacy of all literary creation.

Responses to *Attila* can be read in the handful of reviews it garnered upon its original publication by the Spanish press Destino, and then in a sparsity of subsequent readings. Published in 1991, a year after Coll's death by suicide at age forty-two, in Paris, where he spent his adult life, the novel struggled to find an audience, despite being represented by the powerful Spanish literary agent Carmen Balcells. Rafael Conte, well-known critic for the Spanish newspaper *ABC*, questioned the viability of even discussing such experimental and challenging literature. He praised its boldness while acknowledging the barriers to engagement with it and lamented the lack of connection between author and reader. In a 2011 review, Argentine author Patricio Pron emphasized Coll's eschewing of the norms of traditional storytelling and the ambiguity that resulted from such a departure. While he recognized Coll's audacity, Pron suggested that Coll's pursuit of absolute artistic freedom contributed to his isolation and incomprehensibility. Coll's solitary journey, Pron posited, left him unable to conceive of anyone but himself understanding his work. The abstruseness of Coll's texts, characterized by musicality, vivid imagery, and innovative literary techniques blending medieval epic poetry and twentieth-century avant-garde experimentation, reflects a deliberate intention on the part of the author.

This perspective is reinforced by Coll's own declarations to his closest associates, including Javier Marías, his mentor and friend. Marías, who helped secure the publication of Coll's debut novel in 1982, often referenced him in his own writing. In his obituary for Coll, Marías praised his vast cultural knowledge and literary prowess, but also noted the challenge of Coll's ambitious literary project, which risked being consumed by silence owing to its complexity. Coll's pursuit of a pure literature, akin to Mondrian's revolution in visual art, led him to create works that demand unique interpretive norms, suggesting that only Coll himself held the key to their hidden meanings.

In *Attila*—more so than in *Vitam venturi saeculi*—there are faint glimpses of a plot, such as the section dedicated to the love story of Quixote and Ipsibidimidiata, a romance fraught with obstacles and conflicting loyalties. Yet these plot elements are elusive and fragmented, lack continuity, and often fade into ambiguity. The author's intention is not to construct a coherent narrative but to dismantle the conventional notion of plot, allowing a stream of verbal expression to emerge. This expression is characterized by a tone that swings between elevated and melancholy, punctuated by poetic discoveries and linguistic creations that are often detached from conventional meaning. Although there are occasional moments of clarity, such as those found in Chapter III, these passages do not fully represent the novel's essence. Instead, readers are encouraged to embrace the ambiguity and immerse themselves in Coll's labyrinthine prose, where sparks of intelligence and beauty are found amid the confusion. Throughout the novel, sentences resonate with detail but lack internal coherence, weaving a tapestry of disconnected thoughts that challenge traditional linguistic norms.

Parallels have often been drawn between Coll's writing and that of Beckett or late Joyce. There is, however, a significant difference: even in the case of *Finnegans Wake*, Joyce's final and most challenging work, the author had established a literary precedent that lent credibility to the complexity of his later novels, which serve as a kind of epilogue to a journey of increasing intricacy, where readers choose where they want to enter.

Coll's literary project, by contrast, lacks such a continuum, and menaced him with the risk of total indifference when it came to a readership. Yet his virtuosity and formal rigor cannot be dismissed as mere fireworks. Those who knew him attest that Coll lived in total dedication to his writing and imbued his work with layers of complexity beyond their already formidable challenges. Although he excelled as a translator and produced other, intelligible writings, such as the unpublished essay "Pain, Anesthesia, and Dysthesia," a kind of doctoral thesis for his medical degree, his novels, like *Attila*, reject any semblance of reader engagement. In essence, while he may fall short as a traditional novelist, Coll did so purposefully, guided by an ideal of a literature that exists for its own sake, liberated from any obligation beyond its own abstract expression.

Finding cases of comparable dedication is no easy task. Born to the painter Javier Coll and married to the painter

Lysiane Luong, Aliocha Coll embraced artistic creation in its purest form as his only destiny. He disregarded advice to pursue more accessible or conventional literature, dedicating his talent and entire life to writing, even in the absence of readers. His commitment to experimentation knew no bounds, reflecting an extreme and dark determination that is mirrored in his own books. Consequently, opinions about his work convey a sense of bewilderment: while his literature undeniably possesses value and necessity, advocating for it proves difficult. Imagining that there will future readers who might interpret his books differently is a bold proposition, given that his work fundamentally departs from any previous reading experience.

Yet in the present, we can appreciate the flashes of brilliant prose and the hidden quality that transcends his books while also completing them: the merit in offering a reading experience in which a work of literature is not judged solely on the result it produces, but the process it embodies. It is in this way that Aliocha Coll's unrelenting expression, by nature intrepid and radical, is undoubtedly of artistic value.

JAVIER SERENA

2023

I

LAOCOÖN

And so the misogenesis aborted.

From the thirty thousand child crusaders who set off in search of a taxidermist in 1312.

From the steppe of so sweeping an arch, bigger than the mountains surrounding it. From a basin so intense, deeper than the valleys surrounding the mountains.

From a comedy, which began like this:

SOLOMON

Characters

SPECTER OF ABSALOM
DEAD SON OF A BITCH
LIVING SON OF A BITCH
BAD WHORE
GOOD WHORE
SOLOMON
QUEEN OF SHEBA

Scene I

Specter of Absalom
The unknown denies its supposed opposite

The copula subjects the braggart
The attic and ruin do battle
The name of the highest thing is in its foot
The concave permanent the convex recombable
Quality marriage absolute majority

Dead Son of a Bitch
(*A silence.*)

Specter of Absalom
Do not emerge more weight than cohesion
The least gregarious head carries the herd
Anonymous foundling sips the sea the shore runs to her feet

Living Son of a Bitch
(*Wail mid-silence.*)

Specter of Absalom
The twin names the type
Hawk that errs pigeon stars the ground
The other sky builds cities
Say what you think later think what you say
The moon seems like space
All thought denies all word affirms

The city exceeds its toponymy
Prejudice does not preach

DEAD SON OF A BITCH, LIVING SON OF A BITCH
(*Double silence wail mid-second half.*)

BAD WHORE

Against envy thought
Are is the copula
The dead man and the idiot are
Pain and physics are not
The thought of suffering and god are
Nothing a priori and no god are

GOOD WHORE

Have has the economy
Greater and lesser have
The roof defines the architecture
Not all not have

BAD WHORE

Have does not deny halves

GOOD WHORE

Are does not affirm halves

SOLOMON

Prime laughter? prime judgement
Architecture or pyramid

The sphere does not exist
Symmetry against warmth
The woman appears like the thought
Ethical etymon? ether
All egg? prime physics
Profile measures
Amphinome rage
Star? skin
To face face

SPECTER OF ABSALOM
Substance if superstition

BAD WHORE
Chin nose and lip float

LIVING SON OF A BITCH
Gue gue ga

(EXIT SPECTER OF ABSALOM, BAD WHORE, AND DEAD
SON OF A BITCH.)

SCENE II

GOOD WHORE
Between eros and plow the brow
The trial lasts what the witness does
Agriculture exiles

Stars and clouds
Yes needs other words
Nest breast crest

From an epic poem, URANIA, which began like this:

> still distinct round the earth
> for beautiful free for free perennial
> panthalase and pangea naphthalenes
> for satyriasis parthenogenetic
> brief sun and from your capsized heart
> selfish for being lonely not vice versa
> earth the more wrinkled the younger
> shy for being exposed not vice versa
> under the harvest the darkness

And, further on, continues like this:

> astra extra neuter other
> hiatus placus naught natal
> outside of outside of inside
> musca mosquito of death
> lethal fetus idiot poet
> common aura strange area
> surfaceless mask
> death denizen
> light angel everfalling
> one sex Uranus side
> is flayed fiendish

from monohedral panhedron

From a novel, LAOCOÖN, which began:

Oh Laocoön seer and prophet relegated to impotence for the sons you had and loved, the god who assumed your mind confused your generation with that of the twins you had and I agree with Goethe that one of them, likely Melantho, escaped, at the mercy of your intervention, from the rings of Periboea and I agree with Winckelmann that you needed to revive your battle cry but in order to distort, to your advantage, your countenance that might exercise ophiophagy on your behalf! Oh Laocoön who came to defend your sons in their snake-fighting today everyone knows that reedy Apollo found two pretexts for punishing your love upon your heroic sons since you sent them to found another race of Hercules but they disdained immortality and did not tremble before woman and catapult! Oh Laocoön El Greco was right to paint you at the end of his oeuvre since you illustrate the same message as Prospero and Sarastro the omega the beginning of the future generation the faith in youth and in childhood the Atlas of the future that prism with no edge or roundness which is all his surface! Oh Laocoön dawn of a new noontide the Laocoöntide the equatorial one in which nameless stones and men recognize themselves dawning of a final noon in which the sprig sinks there whence it sprung!

And Laocoön's strength still stands. And Laocoön raised his arms. First his forearms. Then his arms and then his hands.

Covered in tattoos you displayed your torso before a new time with respect to that in which your contemporaries remained outside! Spectators sheltered from the passage of time! Exposed was the plumbing of your dragon-trunk and your veins were verdigris and your mouth a lemniscate with two ophicleids and the native soil was losing your foot! Hanging from serpents your horrifying forehead nose and mouth defended the fruits of your arborescence protected them from your helical tangents serpent of contact but self-generating self-generating I repeat! Unattainable for the group for the quarternity! Diagonal of your sons! Secant line of Euclidian Ophidia! Ink pad of their subjectivities antagonist centrifugal cyclops for a kiss! Teleological pedagogue! And paragogic then! The dental equation a lion's upper dentition and the bottom teeth of a horse! Expression without vibration! Prometheus neither philanthropic nor theomachyan but rather truly in love! Genitors versus tails! Suckable suckers! Everything is success! Even pain is vanity!

Mutation by De Vries when you will come when you will heal the stone of dust that life sickens, sea of dust and skiffs punctured by punctual needles mouthpiece on whistles.

New son progenitor of new shoots our case is not that of individuals but of species our anthropological point of view knows more of Laocoön than your father and less than your son there is a distant son who will know to think about pain whose orgasm will galvanize his thought who will think his pain who will run riot with his thought distant son laughing his head off much more sensible than those who grin!

Oh day! Not, Oh today's place in which yesterday longs for tomorrow! enough.

Oh Laocoön bear in mind that your sons' youth may exgender you. You can congender yourself in it!

Oh today you want to take a surname tomorrow leave your possessions manufactured yesterday suck your thumb and clap your feet until it is wrinkled and they are fingered think with your eyes you will soon hear focus on your nose that your strabismus meets patrona of your face ratio of forehead and profiles the draughty the one of discriminative memory weld your atavisms to your idiosyncrasy weld your logos to your nous smelt your importance your customs tariff-free father smelt your sprouts invent the words of tomorrow lethal to those of yesterday poisonous and you will evolve the new onomatopoeias and hygiene of the verb the extinction of description the perfect future presentation of subjects make the statuary of future, the iconoclast in present, gemonian the rest, forget everything and the canvasses will unhang the sheets will unlink remember must do, before have to do!

Anthophagy is of no use if not to endorse this culture of oralities. How much lives off its overcoat. Like bodies in the void our births fall at the same speed.

Chin and lips correspond to the nose. You wore desert glasses the roundness of the lenses making more of a splash than their smokiness behind those truncated cones your corneas filmed the helmets of the world the inertia of these ephemerals appealed to tomorrow your tricksy pupils abused the dark toward a piece of coal.

Fingertips and hairs against teeth and scales.

When the man stood up the keratin fell.

Antigone assassin who sows your idiosyncrasy in every man history is not a necessity but the homeland writing is still testament it is impossible to write impossible to stop writing poetry has no uncle in America. Neither will ethics come one day when this will be a redundancy! No one speaks some write. The truth is that no one knows their legacy and therefore their language. Fashion decants genius that decants ethics that passes fashion: the Antigone cycle.

Oh gray-less ether oh edge that curves the visuals when will morning dawn where will morning dawn . . . will it evaginate today? will it co-penetrate tomorrow? This is another time the sucker of another necessity.

Toothless Laocoön you seize everything and the furrows of your forehead program your engine action let your feet solidify your waist let your shoulders obey and your neck subjugate them let your hair radiate in a cone, in inverted cone in cone again let your muscles accentuate your symmetry half a body for each twin double body for each amphisbaena! Rotor Laocoön a spider of ash isosceles of thunderbolt! your wrists embalmed your ankles ant-like Laocoön navel-less from your centrifugation.

Go forth and lose yourself so that your children may return. The hero's role is to place oneself outside, to enter the outside, to go and not enter a vehicle, a building, or in the shadow of a work site. Not to go retrojected as Antigone is projected. To go from the beginning and not enter till the end. To go today now and not enter into today forever. The hero is the one who faces the dragon rain the ivy of dew the succulence of the flake the change and the bag of the stone the sworn spectator of the toad and the slug the lighthouse of the centipede. Diameter plus one little extramural dot the hero pockets the ethical dihedron. The last of the Laocoöntids, at night your son will roll the hoop with meridians and dawns to foment the translation of the lands.

There is only one way to love: be perfect. And only ludically can one be perfect.

You don't have horns like Moses but ectopic teeth. On seeing your oarsman hair I confirm you caduceus. Vine mallet. Piteous patricide. Transceluloids. Vacancy.

Pity the most generous people are the most dependent.

Premort premonitory monitor alien do not unheed as teeth strike feet, prosthesis against bunion neither confession nor diary but hypostasis but subtitles. Writing is an occurrence that is to say a digressed recurrence. Death is even. There's always an equal instigator in everything. The person is an importer and the importation. Even with much foreshortening identity does not fit. There is an excess that continues to circle but does not seal. Flaw at every enclosure's center. Assassin cities like Turin cemetery cities like Venice. It's just that the continent is the sea.

Peace is the homeland. Peaces war.

Dies illa upon which Laocoön emerges on the hillock the birth and its flight from the deceased reaches the sun whose half-laughing dawn resolves itself into the sinking night Antigone with no sun sunset you've lost a turn your suspensory bow pursues Laocoön supported by his equine equity geminous is trigeminal love the groan for Antigone the shadowed figure of Laocoön begat the night into the aurora serpent the sky the clouds because they fall too quickly not to become thick and spiraled and in their fulminating pointed ends olé olé olé the sky's tautomachy circular were its horseshoes and the birth the revulsive the unobstructed centrifuge of tangents white bullseye Antigone intersected Laocoön arms against grapevine branches morning not dawned but dawning more and more dawning aspiring in today the quotidian tomorrow tomorrow married to the night macho to the night and the bow shot the horse's mane the horse is male and the other half iris and the tousled hair covered Laocoön's temples zygomas and cheeks without flogging Antigone larval motif uniformly pulls a prank on Laocoön the places have and hold the hypothesis of a monster is the thesis of a god Antigone diametrical with the earth Laocoön sigmoid with heavens what crawled flew and what flew crawled noli me tangere was read on Antigone's soles cyclostome on Laocoön's forehead for all the land in the tropics began the night verbi gratia.

Laocoön told Melantho your future will not be your father's past Melantho replying perhaps the love I have for you will manage to reach me.

Between the settler and the fighting sailor is the incessant training inaccessible premiere.

How to make an ethical *Iliad*?

Dies illa on which trifles and ephemeris show their foundation of epopee the protected tissue that transcends our valid distinction crowns are the small governments of the podocephalus monopod monarch is the world when it turns out it attracts the earth Da Vinci's proportional man

Le Corbusier's scale and Penfield's opponent at that hour when the horizon is embroidered with festooned half-dawns and you remain in your place like a cornered convict and wherever you move the center moves with you objective accomplice of the court and of you when golds herald sunset of a meridian hemisphere behind the sun gone forever in the chronic ocean abyss and the man loses the blueprint of his body in the fall when the water when the water storms not sparingly but in an eruption boiled in its own gush and loses itself in the heavens increasingly and absolutely separate just as cosmically united verbi gratia the earth be the most generous of astral bodies ethical atom there are no Urania and Demeter weaving finger poetry Antigone lacks the tendon the phoenix fails to convince Laocoön.

Red summer bombyx remaining in the cocoon you made of yourself you stay in yourself you die in yourself winter spring and autumn one after another.

Da capo ostensive contingencies war births civil law and the metropolis castles nothing sprouts without weapons everything killed while killing the lynx saw that the eagle watched a rolling skull bewitched song to travel and awaken and travel waking up and travel not waking up in every man there is a viper and a wise monkey with a mirror symbionts produce mythology logolysis blurs the protogram, geriatrician of neologisms, it's convenient to dance because the friendship between arms and legs can introduce the head to sex the pig's pain has tiger faces and the worm's has the faces of a pig fast trochoidal folds cascades of parallel folds no leaf was falling it was two alternated faces.

Dies illa! Illa and its anchoring noontide its geminated hemicrania its effeminated syncope and its geminated hemicrania its effeminated syncope and its effeminated syncope! Dies illa! and its get up bite dragons watch the weapons of the suicidal man the one who does not lead himself to safety novice stone among lichen and soot maimed animals loosen the border the lameness of domestics is another ferociousness evil did start off winged nor did it crawl it followed if evil is not pain in terms of action saving the name of pain for the effect then evil is just a category spear lance and helmet weapon against the city the woman against the walls crow's nests and cups Noah's ark Trojan horse the post-diluvian rainbow the death of Astyanax blood and iron taste the same the heart and fist are cubed the same against attrition bracelets against hoops smothering more adapt the attack to the antagonist than the defense to the protagonist who prefers to feel the shape by weight? the lesser age does not adapt and it's not that the age of man adapts to the lesser age but rather the lesser age adapts the age of man whoever tears the sword from the hand will clang the anvil the age of man is affiliated the vanity of man is more childish than that of a woman everything played is learned and everything learned is eventually done that is to say it is won or lost moorings or nooses anchor or purse the city occupied the center of an era of powder extramural sweat and intramural urine cone-shaped roofs of the Renaissance make the sky heavy tragedy staccato dawn of death its smile chipped the horizon even on the summas sea there are two horizons to say book says on a trip to write always deals with today and never here come naked and laurel-crowned men among the cypresses with regard to the sky man is dactylated, by definition the law and alphabet exclude each other freedom is the remainder of dividing the possible among vested interests austerity and humor marry verbi gratia "The Fable of Polyphemus and Galatea" the thickness of their arms covered the outlines of their chest and their fists each buttock were worth kouros centripetal of torso in rhombus by the basilisk gaze by the Orphic smile the passing of profile came to be the passing of forehead to childhood cheeky age not of myth but of ludic logos the emphasis of the most tortuous thing is the straight thing and the emphasis of the straight thing is the most diagonal thing nothing departs without its vengeance on shoulders coincidence abandons the age of man the sword is the greatest premise of reason celestial rain the other sex is past the present is the reiterated past medicine is past it is backward that the dragon terrorizes me, how to get in front of it? its eye washes itself like a cat.

While the first laocoönite considers Russian roulette the last antigonite rolls dice.

Rage is the refusal to renounce.

A hemisphere for every man.

The woman phenomenally sufficient.

From BABEL, VERTEX, using the following alphabet: a e i o u w y b ch d f g(u) j k l m n ñ p r s t v x z,

h

plrkafvfjsibyeywiiysxgxsgxotdvzbfaylssusw otuwñachbpmbnjbenuewklrvrrir

II

ATTILA

Morris column invaginated in Omphalo. Fall into the hole to begin reading its only sign. Emerge to finish reading it. The omphalic slope selected the signatory's name. Some suggested Tiresias, others Hippolyta or Penthesilea. Someone whispered Attila. The point being that it was announced:

Horses charged against the suspended dust and hastened it beneath their hooves. From their mothers the colts received instructions to knead. The horses charged against the dust cloud and turned it into ground. With respect to the steppe they were a herd, but with respect to the horses the herd formed the star that shone, lone but all, in the embossed ring of its flooding rays.

Horses charged monastic against the blush pursued by cannibal horses. The dust could not hide in the gloaming nor the wolf in the dust. Addendum:

Major: The horizon distinguishes all quadrupeds.

Minor: But the zenith confuses quadrupeds and bipeds.

Medium: Love is the school of privileges and freedom is the privilege of this school.

"Of those who love us we only feel loved by those we love. The love of the others is sigilegion," thought the little father, great son, and woman. The willow wept and the aspen quaked. The water nymph fluttered. The saurian's tail broke off and snaking its way upstream it went in search of its tongue. Isis, dumbfounded, had come across a janeirean phallus. Thus rose the morning, following a night when the moon had rekindled mourning and the candles the veil, it rose from the east and from the seer, and both middays converged in the clef of a crescent and snowcapped arch.

(Of the many we love we only feel loved by those who do not love us, said the siphon to the echo)

The stranger, the well-loved, the one with no horse or tent or yarmulke or rug, was called Attila Historia. He had a son, who renounced his name to change his surname, so instead of Quixote Historia, he was called Hydattila Utopia. This bit of ingenuity allowed for a celestial novel, and thus these pages recount the survey of love between two men and between the most modern of the ancient names of one of them and the oldest of the new surnames of the other.

Fleeces of amethyst gas, ripped from green chaparral by the western blush, pirouetted gracelessly in their ascent toward the rust, where an oscillating breath vaporized old blood clots. In its insoluble sulfur, the turquoise-toned sky acted as broiler, which heightened the bitterness of that mired opal. A rose-pink cirrus hung down, more spoiled than broken.

And restive surface, the promiscuous foreign neighbor could not eddy through any of its tracks in order to escape, turncoat, from the black, given the ivory buoy that prevented it from sinking into the abyss: and thus, the boiled ink intensified the steeping of that nacreous fisheye. And all this pestilence, prisoner of its nausea, seemed to filter down from its stroppy center, frosted fussiness. Only at the limit of a horizon hoisted with grappling poles and pulleys was another, tramontane execution skeptically espied. As if the crests of the ocean floor emerged and the sea's only surviving motion was its plunge toward greater depths, so that its whole light was beached and spray under water, and thus the elements rebelled against their own gravity as well as the firmament's scorn: rotor skeleton made external to skin and evaginated viscera boasting of seams: marble bubbles solidary even in their exultation trampled the flora above the ether and from that stonecut press conical streams of paradise flowed unaided from the flattened fauna. So only at the edge of another horizon reduced by ashen fogs did a bell tower attempt to crystallize atop a stump of scales and sand.

The valley sweated light. The smallholdings played blind man's bluff with two scarves. The westerly wind inspected the treetops and they, yielding slightly, spilled some of their foliage. But the zephyr fanned those trees that burned in summer. Some cherry trees appeared to be in both bloom and fruit, and the flower and the fruit seemed to patch the cherry trees, citrifying one without the other. The slope, on its knees, became border. Aeolian aspens concealed lubriciously their little disputes. And the supple light made sequins on those fringes, which ran back and forth in single file. The warm and groggy earth gave itself over to the plow, which, naked, rose through her like two twin and antagonistic rivers. East besieged with diamond squadrons of fallow furrows and rows of birch. Two farmhouses interred the twinkling of starry burials. Feral trees preferred ravines to roads, while a duo of almond trees jumped the basin bed. Farsighted hordes of oak groves contemplated those lands brighter than peaks, airier than craters. And so corralled, the georgic valley issued emissaries like a man's eye on a woman's hair. And through the highest pass the bloodless sky descended to beg indolence from the granite.

Some distance from the crag, the circumambient cloud grimaced with constriction. The rock burst into fans, as if Pelion had splayed out in its womb. From black ribs sprouted pines in orderly dispersion extending toward the valley, halted only by the sun's august breath as it drowned in the high straits of the decaying glacier. Wisps of clouds fell in the neighboring east, catapulted by the afterglow, futile parabola of violent redemption, for at the end of the valley of secretion, the saurian was not current but the tiger repellent, its back rooms and hindquarters aflame, and its scorpioned tail keeping in airy suspense the luciferous dust and the usurial dust, its shuttering flanks awaiting only the visual, or meridian, through serrated toothy tendons, the front quarters and head of the beheading face smudged by ire, that of nadir. Meanwhile, the more hopeful trees neither stood rooted nor walked but were like windborne merry-go-rounds, children, spinning in a grassy clearing whose venial aftermath stacked the heroes' somber tombstones on its borders, rising more comically than tragically and more comic for their accumulation. Between tiger and merry-go-round, stealthily and in the Egyptian style, turf and two small trees avoided the shadow of the experimental terror.

Lone sails of Phoenician galleys floated in an unseemly sky, all unfurled, and turgid and contiguous they advanced without pilfering the wind, serially tucking the land into their shadows, and only a lake multiplied them, the absence of eyelids like scales. In the dense sea of the cismontane ocean depths, fortified cities danced in whirlpools, like posted bottles of casus belli, the inertia of the container opposed to the inertia of the contents, while in the gentlest part of the valley small forests ravaged by light and perspective vied to pass themselves off as fields of wheat. Indifferent to land, sea, and air two manured embankments emerged from consubstantial ground, creating a crossing from path to path. An oak tree died upside down from its leaves, bent over the Spanish saddle of a mule that tried to rise on its hind hooves without afrightening those who seemed to be held up by its erect and anticipatory ears, ears more face than the fork of enucleated contours, serrated with an irrepressible crown. The horse, tether of fate, white as the cloth cut from Attila's shroud, hung from the figure of a forespilt rider with the axle of the landscape in the hand of an extended right arm. With lycanthropic eyes, the horse watched the mule. The rider hung from the axle of the landscape. This axle braced itself on the other figure, perplexed in the air, the hand armed and the head hairtorn. Along the bank of the efferent road fled the trunks of two maples, without folia or radices, crossed in a lemniscate, one forespilt and the other straight, both thundergenic.

Behind the figure on foot was dazzled sky and the ruin of a triumphal arch, a so-called bridge between a pile of towers with open windows looking onto the heap of walls with open niches, piles different from the sky only by emphasizing the tangled weeds, and a wall conceived on crustless ground, which never finished being born of this supernal hell, crossed with itself beyond its circle. Suspicion of a riverbed of paths. The knee behind the grounded figure was a gully whose sloping sides the lithographically set square sky made moldy, and a citadel, a citadel-derived preterit, revenge, always of absence, another iterative presence, and a marbling sky. Fresh cliff drop, stumbling intact, downstream without flow went another arch, the alternate arch.

The earth must be serene in order to reflect the serenity or disturbance of the sky. And the earth is earth, water of the earth, and vapor of the earth and its water. And the earth was serene under the sky, and the figures were on the earth. That day the earth and all the vapor were shadows, shadows of today, shadows of today's shadows, shadows of the shadows of today's shadows, shadows of the shadows of the shadows of today's shadows. And today the water is that of the wind which, with combustive and burning light, sets the sun and the crowns of trees and retracts to the cloud and the bird.

Turning his back to the valley he crossed the azure pass. The pale pink glow spindled overhead. The azure marshes now salamanders among storm clouds resisted urine-greening as in lamprey-mouth beams the muck liquefied hot dung from bulls' bowels. A clever shroud screened the sunset and unscreened significant parts of the figures, horrible fits geminating more horror, instantaneous movements in evidence of madness. Suspended Pisan shafts of cyanoclasic capitals. And the flayed valley bled, over knoll and under pond, through the reed-less canes. Canoes of shroud rags sailed down the valley.

The figure's halo is and was light absorbed in dust, absolved in smoke. And the smoke was that which spewed fire, vomit of smoke in the smoke, from the viscera between its orifices inexorable decanting of the detaining contents, not a fire that builds ruins, but a fire that destroys novelties, ruins surrounded by lilies, orange trees, and birds, round rounded by monkeys. And it is and will be the figure's halo a twilight of heat lightning, parabolic in the heavens on the horizon, zigzagging in the lacuna, terrestrial heat lightning at the zenith of the sky, nadir of celestial earth. Flash from heat lightning from the nadir of celestial earth layer of uranium eggs, and inverse pyramids. Earth more celestial than the sky and more marine than the sea surrounded by fountains, orange trees, and lilies, round rounded by corpulent angels. In the last zag of heat lightning, the figure is the halo of the other figure. The figure looks from the halo that was to the halo that will be. The other figure looks at the halo that was.

There are three skies: the first sky, the reverse of the first sky, and the second sky. The first sky, spelunking, sips the smoke and the dust, the soot and the urine, and like a suction cup, raises earth to earth, winged terraces that spiral, city rivers that climb the mountains, water rivers that descend to the valleys, the reverse side of the first sky, spooked, that fires from one bolt to another, with bolts, sky, that make embossed rags creak, patchwork scraps of an unfinished dome, unfinishable tin edge, preserves pecked open and snatched from outside, cutting, reverse of the first sky wounded from the second sky, and potentially mutilating the earth and yearning to mutilate the first sky, mutilating wound edges, more than weapon edges, the sound effectist, the illuminator, the rationalizer of green, the sky responsible for the earth's light, the green light, and for its nine colors, the conical colors, the intestine, the assassin, the mansion, the malletine, the fericircine, the archpristine, the domino, the ipsinterino, and the assassin's neighbor, among which converge antish figures clothed, nude, and seminude, which swarm with rods to the water rivers and ebb with candles from the city rivers, myriad at the head and tail, with witnesses to its equinity, more water pegasus than air, the horse will not rise through the void in the reverse of the first sky nor will the centaur through the other, the second sky, speculating.

But from common course, the tip of the figure's shoe was fish, and the fingers on his hand were lion's mane, circumscribed to a man's face, with setting iris on his eyebrow and on his lips rising teeth, and the back of the other figure's skull was a bird and his middle finger a dart.

The least rugged profile, the flow of a figure, is rocks in ladders and rocks on sloping surfaces, bifurcated at the head and corresponding at the heel, buttresses of a figure's most rugged profile, the diligence, sickles point up against the wind, cutting the wind in a straight line, and in uniform continuity, sickles point downward against the earth, cutting the earth in parabolas, and the edges of each parabola are male teeth and female nails. Both profiles of a hyperbola, which by hyperbole identifies one figure with the other, the other figure that is the landscape that shapes the hollow of an opened door. And a city gives shape to the crust of the opened door. Nearer hyperbole, the earth is metric. Beyond hyperbole, the earth is a canopy of formless profiles. Indeed, one figure could be the other if the heads were not also haloed within.

There are three cones. The cone of the earth, the cone of the air, the cone of the water. In the cone of the earth weighs a full and muffled moon, it counterweighs the sinister obliquity of bridges, ports, footbridges, and fords, obliquity of the spears and torches that pass, passing and passing, floating with men clustered in their supporting regiments, men with oblique-soled feet, who turn right to left. And the river wants to levitate, the aspens too, those that neither weigh nor counterweigh, inertia-less mass, same as the obliquity, here, sinister, always, the sinister is here, in this cone, moon with its muffled and full reflection in the notch of the effluvial cloud, cloud whose inner rings don jewels to immortalize its core and strip the outer rings. The one that passes to earth through the murder of today, that reptilian affair that dispatches each fluid to its reflection in another fluid, leg with less stamina the more it runs, illusion of passage of the earth through the symmetry of identical fluids, to another cone. Hodiecide passage, since all its reflections are oblique, and all its diagonals sinister. The cone of the air, fellator of the earth, the invisible cone, cone of the night, even at noon, the leaden one, whose position no other resists, the one that stops at an angel's distance and inhales the earth, whose layers rise with creasing, the lifting first and then the creasing of conical fellation, this is the shelter of the support, occlusion of perspective, pleating of the pure position, of earth's unconditional situation, of location foreshortening without escape, pleats of ecstasy, which cannot be without space, and there is no pleat-less space. The cone of water, the auricular, the prancing, antennal, the one of echo and dream, of pots and rattles, and of hats, the antispheric, that is, of the curved dihedral, of the plow of revolution, that leaves the earth without passage or passion, depressed, drownable. May it be noted that between the cones of water and air, precisely between the cone of water and the cone of earth fellated by the cone of air, a translucent egg contains a man and two twin men, lantern of itself.

Firs sparkle in the snow. Saxifrage buttonholes the mountains. The ladder trims the slopes. If the frame is on the canvas, the earth on the terrace, where mountain competes with volcano. Courtyard among skyscrapers, for swallows' swoops. Scrape, sky, the trees are brushing. Through the softness of night lightning cleaves. Through its cleft the night grows tender. Silhouette of a stilt house, two indoor men converse with the murmur of a cypress stream. Bitonal murmur, worn and docile, staggered and sustained.

Clouds and mountains play leapfrog. The cascade skips rope with the bridge. The lowest reflections and the highest sheen between the intertwined silhouettes of both.

And the branch a folding screen.

The summit lifts the mountain's skirts. The river ejects the valley. The walker's tear washes the foot or marks the trail. How many figures fit? The one who sees, the one who looks, and the convoy of the one who looks. Beasts of burden guide the gaze. But from sight are the summit saucers and rivers. The tear that marks the path gradually creates a bed. The tear that washes the foot quickly creates a flow. Even the most depressed valley is the son of cliffs. The only ones running the rotation are the trees. The eagle's nest does not catch meteorites. Doesn't Nature tell art that the profile passes before the face?

Compass rose. Rose of identities. Storm of skies. Storm of identities. Sky of national flags, sportive. Sky of family shields, professional, ludic. Sky of coins, metallic, commemorative. Sky of advertising stamps, propagandist. Sky of shirts, social, metempsychotic. Sky of big-headed feet, of walking sticks or masks, unblockers, recoilers. Sky of triumphal trophies, of invented taxidermists. Sky of abscissa registers. Sky of skeins, polyurethanes, undeveloped. Sky of autophagous dodecaters by tautobolics and autobolics by tautophages. Sky of incused soles. Sky of cosmometers, antifernales, recluses. Sky of drowned relics slaked by arrogated lawyers. Sky of the manumitted, furniture for cripples, property for soldiers. Sky of navy and black satin with sequins in red lace. Sky of sea hourglasses and beach water clocks. Sky of snowy basilisks, sublimated by salty jellyfish, and of monsters muffled in statues' garb. Sky of griper's coals, cataclysmic blotch. Sky of ghosts, sloth of the spirit that slows. Sky of jealousy (ensuring no love can protect us from the truth). Sky of stains, folded. Sky of driving caves, support wheels. Sky of prone deployments to supine reflections. Sky of grown extracts or blown details, of tetrahedrons, and two men in each of them, and one man in every two of them, hostages of each woman, of another woman every woman and so every man. And so the men in each of them said letters, and the man in every two of them said "What shall I call you? You? Your you, more my me than the original version of my memory? What shall I call you, half that never begets symmetry, but always homothety? Half alone only, and half alone accompanied by your homothety. Ipsibidimidiata? No. Thalia. For between ear and mouth you think. Between mouth and ear you smile. And between ear and mouth and mouth and ear you laugh."

III

THE HUN AND THE OTHERS

The ultramarine sky thickens
     And the ultraterrestrial sea.
The night is diced by another sky
     And the sea dusted.
So patterned your dress, washerwoman
     Who leaks on the beach.
The widow catches fire in the stars
     And the soul in the pupils.
The steam makes gray that mourning
     That whitens upon turning in to bed.
And the bride's veil spends the night
     With the smoke of home.
The winking eye is crying
     As the dunes run.
Who turns his back behind the screen?
     The muffled autumn.
Who embosses the black armor?
     The misted valley.

Who hammers the genuine stud
        In this fishless pot?
Multiplying one's own presence
        By the common absence
And repeating its fleetingness
        On the urban consistency
To the fated they give fate
        And to fortune summons
To the lovers testimony
        And antimony to the poet
Giving directions to the banished
        And meaning to the buried
They bore the domesticable place
        Of those who make home
So that someone else wants to die in it
        And someone else wants to be born.
What eye senses the sideral humor?
        What ear understands the earth?
Uncover the foreign and veil the near
        Since the halo is one
The earth takes shape on the moon
        Measuring various beats
The halo sheaths all limits
        Luminous tortillon
The black halo of each star
        The one that shines inward
The widest rhythm is that of air
        And the strangest too
The intermediate rhythm is that of water

And the medium too
That of the earth is the most frequent
The least wide too
The rhythm of those beats' halo
Nimbus limbo beat
Spiral that traverses and embraces
The chalk and pool
Numbers that chalk names that fill with water
The path and the detour
Revealing more magic on the roof
Than on the overlap
And understanding the deposit in what is loose
And not the exhibition
Not the exhibition of the right-hand shadow
Nor the left-hand shadow
Not eastern exhibition of the shadow
Nor western exhibition
But waning at the origin deposit
And waxing at the end
Deposit that wanes in adherence
And grows in release
Avoiding the exponent slander
Of the shadow in the night
Approximate proximity is the day
Between sun and earth
Presented distance is the night
Between sky and sea
Let each one pick its hour of love
Each shall have its place

Does it count that the sea and the sun are antipodean
If the stars enter the cave?

Quixote did not reply with a hendecasyllable, but with a kiss on the lips. Ipsibidimidiata anchored his head between her hands. After a while, Quixote covered them with his own and, holding them, pulled them away from his face and placed them on his knees. Ipsibidimidiata rested her face on them. "What doubt can there be," she said. "Urania will always be Mnemosyne's beloved daughter, because she is the Muse of love par excellence."

They remained thus for several hours, she sleeping and he on watch. He very carefully removed one hand and waved off the mosquitoes. The September night made orange the marble terrace, but the marble on the staircase was a thing of oleanders in bloom. Ostia stretched to the sea. And the sea stretched from Ostia. And that was the sense, as if all the space there was determined by Rome's knee, and even the breeze only changed direction and force according to Rome's breath. In the port lions recently arrived from Utica roared, but not hale roars directed at a target, but echoing as if in a spiral, uttered in a paradoxical dream, fending off the fate sucked from that orgiastic athleticism. Unsubtractable. That was the worst. Not the inability to add something new to that environment, but that nothing could be subtracted. For just as the lion keeps its claws and tail away from its jaws, so Rome not only closed its doors to its troops but also to its broadcast support, to the gargantuan machinery whipping up the dust. And the world was at the gates.

The day had not yet dawned when from the port other sounds arose. Chains and crates. Ipsibidimidiata woke and straightened her torso and head as a piece like a needle, slow and continuous, on a scale. The left side of her face was marked by Quixote's fingers and knuckles. She blinked her eyes forcefully and rubbed her numbed temple and cheek. They smiled at each other . . .

Easily she jumped like a top spinning on marble and tugged at Quixote's wrists.

"Wait, my hands and one leg are asleep!"

"Come on, lazybones," and she pulled with all her might, leaning back on her heels.

"What cheek!!"

Ipsibidimidiata sensed he was about to get up and, releasing him, took to running as if in flight. He accepted the provocation but after three strides his leg sunk into a furious anthill and he had to content himself with walking. She had already surrendered fully to the pure pleasure of the chase when she left the terrace and began climbing the gentle slope, passing through a cluster of tamarisk, that lead to the peristyle's outer gates.

"Ah! Quixote!" Her feet traded wings for shovels when, a few meters away, the half-seen heft of a tawny dog blocked her path, looking at her with reptilian eyes and gulping saliva.

Quixote arrived in pieces: first the head, pulled by the ears, then the arms with a leg in each hand, the heart and lungs vying not to be last.

"It's nothing but a goat!"

Ipsibidimidiata seemed to be staring at her own vision, as if to define it further. Slowly her incredulous mouth abandoned the square for the circle . . . and at last she looked squarely at Quixote.

"I thought it was Luperca."

While the two laughed, the goat, as unperturbable as a fig tree, resumed its suppression of the shrub, not deviating one inch from its path.

They entered the house from the rear. "I'm so thirsty," said Ipsibidimidiata when she reached the atrium, then disappeared.

But the returning steps measured another determination, very different.

With "Rome requires your presence without delay," the emissary's voice replaced his final footfall. In the weak blue of the lacial dawn, the folds of the man's tunic turned him to a column.

"I will leave once I have rested," Quixote replied, taking his right fist into his left palm.

The emissary left the atrium with the same speedy diligence as a piece leaves the checkerboard. The household descended on Quixote. He ordered that a horse be saddled for him and, after composing his spirits with a deep breath, retired.

The wind knows well that the sail is more powerful than the wall, even if the sea gives it more runway than the land. The rain knows well that thin grass is more powerful than a thick dam. And so, Attila's tent crackled with more wisdom than rage. Inside, the torch flames appeared ensconced in balloons, and their axes did not provide them with fuel, but only support. With one leg extended and the other bent to support the arm of the hand where he rested his chin, Attila mused: "The rhetorician informs me that Quixote doesn't have much left to learn, his understanding of the language and its Classics has been so swift and perfect . . . but a constant and impertinent vice mars that building, and that is that every time he should say 'and,' Quixote says 'is,' regardless of the sentence or context, making no exception ever, to the point that it seems to be, for him, a rule as inflexible as it is aberrant . . . No one else has reported this eccentricity to me. What could that mean? Does he do it deliberately, just to provoke those pedants? . . . or . . . rather than the joke of an insolent student, might it not be a critical game, an acerbic picking at the subordinative structure of the imperial language . . . ? I'll have to ask him . . ."

"Letter from Rome!" rang a voice outside. Thereupon an archer on watch entered the tent and stood by the entrance, awaiting instructions.

"Bring me the missive, and see to the man and the horse," commanded Attila.

The warrior left as if entering a cave to hunt and promptly returned with his loot, turning and exiting in the same manner.

Attila read carefully only a few of the lines, or rather, a few of the between-the-lines. "Hmm . . . distrusts Byzantium . . . proposes an alliance . . . suggests a vast campaign with an initial expedition in Thrace before the next winter . . . I see the trap, I won't walk into its mouth. My interest lies in remaining north of the two cities, occupying the center of Europe in a diffuse but consistent manner, and not leaving such my position unless it is to attack both cities simultaneously. But to wait and do nothing is most prudent and effective. Watch and be prepared . . . Against me, Byzantium 'is' Rome, as Quixote would say."

He clapped loudly and immediately a servant dressed in the Greek fashion appeared. "Prepare to leave tomorrow for the Empire. Go secretly to Ostia and convey the following to Quixote: be alert regarding Rome, and that I await him here as soon as possible. Go." The Greek made a slight bow and exited without turning his back.

Attila returned to his thoughts. "Yes, his assimilation into Roman culture is marvelous. With him here, Rome is more a hostage than I am with him being there. My steppe-son holds the heart of the lycanthropic city . . ."

A horse's whinny sounded, clipped and shrill. The horse, stepping sideways, cast its profile in relief on the tent, first in full view and then obliquely. The man on the ground pulling the reins succeed in disengaging the gait.

The Tiber somewhat cleared its waters, and again braids of its current shone. But the salt in the air didn't seem the least bit healthy for the marshes, which without hesitation continued returning only part of the light. Fortunately, the olive trees, less sparse and mournful than those of Bohemia, settled all debts with the sky. "Why is so much metal in the Aeolian mirror?" wondered the Greek rider, and remembered that the more civilizing gods were skilled warriors, and great predators of titans, nymphs, and satyrs. "Yes, the olive and the laurel, celestial, collect the light tax on valleys and rivers, burnishing peace and elegy . . ."

Shadows inverted, Quixote saw this landscape while following the Tiber upstream on the opposite bank, but it wasn't this view that occupied his mind, already worried. Only the Aventine Hill managed to alter his introspection. Quixote went to his steed, but, finding himself on the right bank of the river, had to go around the hill to head toward the Porta Portese. From the other side of the Tiber came the smell of the emporium, an inextricable mixture of aromas and fetor that had taken possession of the air, another case of a vehicle alienated by the permanence of its contents. He crossed the Ponte Sublicio and climbed the Palatine.

A groom at the gate came out to meet him. Quixote dismounted and accompanied by a Praetorian escort, entered the palace. In the brief time he had to wait, several men came out of the imperial hall, some important figures and others nobodies, but their value was the will delegated to them, which they embodied effectively.

The moment he entered the hall, Rome came to him, and with an affability that emphasized his majesty, took him by the arm before he could effect the slightest bow. Light seemed to be entering there from everywhere, white light, as if midday were lying down and around. They took a few steps until, behind the circle of light, Quixote spotted the Field of Mars at the foot of the Pincian Hill, the greenest of the city.

The discreet pressure he felt at his elbow invited him to make a quarter turn and come face to face with Rome. "How is Ipsibidimidiata?"

"Your daughter is splendid."

They took a few more steps together, but more slowly. "How long has it been since you last returned to Etzelburg?"

"Fifteen years, Rome," Quixote answered, unhesitating in his accounting.

"I wonder if your father will recognize you. You are the envy of the young patricians . . . No, no! Don't look so modest, you know it's true . . . When you came here, how old were you? Three? . . . yes, more or less, wearing wolfskin over your shoulder and craving macerated meat, which was repulsive to your tutors. And now? Our poetry and our law hold no secrets for you . . . and I would bet my best charioteer that you can tell apart the different grapes of the Empire. What do you make of that?"

"Rome, I was never the same enterprise at three years old that Roman children are. Like my peers, I already rode horses and shot with a bow, knew how to hunt, knew the patience of hunting. I already knew Mundzuk's language. The nightly monologues, which poured their meanings into each other in a fraction of a second of their intercurrence, I understood them. The polyphony of the day, and its spiral of repeated and difficult elements, I intercepted it . . . And I remember my grandfather's words in the twilight, illusions in vertical zigzag . . . speaking to me of a dust ocean, the pristine witness of the east, beyond which there were no monsters or surfacing from Tartarus like in yours, but another empire of poetry and law, hedonistic and armed . . . And I heard him recount how we had come to save it, how our culture had put right that decadent civilization, how our natural law had healed its civil law in the midst of total corruption, how our cosmic poetry had dissected its chronic mannerisms ... and then, then we returned to our origins, to that free and immediate projection of the sky onto the earth ..."

Rome's eyes studied Quixote's pupils anxiously with brief, abrupt star-like flashes, as if trying to dilate them in order to delve into the feelings and moods breathing life into his inspired soliloquy. Quixote immediately felt the violence and impudence of that gaze, and fell silent, not out of embarrassment but letting it be, pretending to do so out of respect, not to bore his distinguished interlocutor.

Rome raised his left hand and instantaneously the wine-pourer came to them, serving them a cup of Falernian and returning to his hidden spot in the hall.

"I have decided to entrust you with a position in the administration of the Empire," said Rome soft but surely, as they looked out over the Capitol and the Forum.

Quixote knelt but had hardly grazed the tile when Rome gestured for him to rise. He gave him another penetrating look, but this time with a measure of affection.

"Is Ipsibidimidiata still writing poetry?"

"More than ever, Rome."

Arm outstretched, Rome's left hand came to rest on Quixote's right shoulder, a sign that the audience was over. Quixote withdrew, head and shoulders deferential.

"The Empire's heart is in the cardinal points of its borders, and the city is nothing more than its wrinkled skin," Rome mused again, turning back to the window. "Quixote is not even an imperial subject. I have no doubt that he loves our world. But where does his heart truly lie? Is this all his love? And why? What margin of trust can I have in him? I must test his loyalty and stimulate his interest in the Empire at the same time. And the best way is to give him a role . . . As for his status as a hostage, I rely more on Ipsibidimidiata than on all explicit surveillance . . . Yes, little binds us as much as the origins of the things we love and, even more so, of the person we love."

Outside, between the Carinae and the Suburra, a Christian procession advanced slowly toward the Esquiline gate. Behind it, Quixote saw the cross looming overhead and thought, surprising himself, "what a fundamental symbol of evil, since does it not cardinally associate the empire with pain? Yes, cardinally, possession and suffering?" He crossed the street and entered the Forum of Nerva.

"From head to toe, the sun grows and shrinks, and from side to side the moon waxes and wanes . . . So that the sun always returns but the moon comes and goes. And thus the sun is regenerated on its own, but the moon is reborn. So that noon always celebrates the origins, but the new moon celebrates the origin, and the full moon celebrates the ending . . ."

"The things you come up with!" exclaimed Quixote, embracing Ipsibidimidiata from behind and pressing his left cheek to her right. They heard the synchronous pulse in their temples and in their free ears the crickets' same rhythm, a pulsing of love in concert with a rhythm of heat. Through the grooves of the peristyle, Sirocco-scraped grains of sand ran like the organs of irreversible hourglasses bearing witness to completely random time.

"What did that Greek want?" asked Ipsibidimidiata.

"How long had he been waiting for me in Ostia?"

"Since you went to Rome. He arrived the evening of the day you left."

"Three days . . . He came with a verbal message from my father. He wishes for me to present myself in Etzelburg as soon as possible."

"Why so much secrecy, and why a verbal message?"

"You know that, in principle, I am a hostage agreed upon by our parents."

An external silence followed these words, but both lovers heard the raucous inner turmoil of the other.

"And my father has just proposed some role in the Empire for you . . ."

"Yes . . ."

"What does Attila want? What do you plan to do? . . ."

They raised their faces to separate their violent pulses.

"For the time being, to go to Etzelburg. Immediately. What is unbearable is the doubt, and how it subjugates us with this ominous apprehension. The sooner I find out what he wants, the sooner we will know what to expect. And this is what matters now."

Ipsibidimidiata held back her blinking in order to contain the emergent tears. But the glints of veiled candlelight did not go unnoticed by Quixote, who nestled the magnificent polygonal oval of her face in his hands.

"Don't cry. Nothing can separate us. You and I are united in the end already. Although our origins are different. Although now they diverge."

"But they haven't passed. Our origins are present. What if they come into opposition? What if they become enemies?"

"They are in the present. But all that is origin is not end, and everything that is end is not origin. They have nothing to do with us."

This time Ipsibidimidiata's tears spilled, not as discrete tears but in a curtain. She cried in silence, her expressive face writing in Quixote's eyes that she did it out of anguish, reassurance, and lyricism.

They left the house for the field behind. The sky seemed to tuck the night over the earth and they felt bundled up by the horizons. But, making sure the other didn't notice, each looked to the east, conjuring it.

And so they didn't see it, that behind their heads two falling stars crossed paths, emblematically.

Leaving Aquileia behind, Quixote ventured into the Julian Alps, a cross rib of gorges and ravines in which the south lost its way as did the north, a sage study of a peony center on a chrysanthemum line. Then he let himself be collected by that second noon in Europe, the southern basin of the Danube, and, three days passed, he thought he recognized that flood of grass where the Carpathians ran aground.

Three droves of horses surrounded Etzelburg, all carefully watched and attended to. The colts and breeding mares on the outside, the horses in the middle, and inside the milking mares. An immense mosaic of carts and hanging clothes converged obliquely on Attila's tent. The tribal chiefs resided on the periphery, as they were directly responsible for the horses. Attila's own tribe was responsible for the care and protection of his tent and the outer herd. If a stranger appeared, it was at their discretion whether or not they were admitted, but if they were, the chief of the nearest tribe was to be alerted. He would then provide part of the escort, proportionate to the emissary's importance.

Under these conditions, Quixote entered Etzelburg, though personally accompanied by the tribal chief corresponding to his point of arrival, an honor reserved for kings and princes of the highest rank.

He entered the tent alone, and he felt he was dreaming a memory. Attila was at its center, standing, guardian of the absence of something that, even present, would not be recognized. Quixote walked toward his father, quickening his pace, and when he was two steps away, his father came forward and embraced him. No word spoken, they sat down together on a bench, at two opposite stripes of a star of sewn wolfskins that stretched between them.

Attila looked at him, satisfied. There was nothing for him to ask. And without further ado, he began his speech. "My grandfather led us here providentially. The cities of the West are dying, and their Imperial well is exhausted. We have waited sixty years, and the time has come to intervene. But we will not make the mistake of yore, the Oriental error. We will not occupy this Empire or fill its cities. We will avoid all replacement. Scrupulously. No. What we will do, what I have already been preparing, is to harvest the classical legacy. One world is dying, and another is being born. Yes, we have come here at the right time. For we will also harvest the Christian promise. And we will withdraw. Yes, yes, you heard me correctly, we will withdraw. To instill in our culture and in Nature those ingredients, and not the reverse, as we have done until now. We will withdraw to the meadow with a civilization without cities and a culture without doctrines, and we will build a new tradition, abandoning the sumptuous carrion of the Empire to the jackals that circle us . . . That was my plan when I married your mother, and when I accepted that you and all the sons of my chiefs would leave as hostages for Rome and Constantinople, when I surrounded myself with the Empire's most eminent sages. The plan for a natural civilization and a classical culture for our people . . ."

Affectionate, Attila smiled. "I can tell you have matured. Your education is excellent. All the reports concur . . . And you have realized, I am sure, what is brewing in Europe, the eternal opposition of a classical civilization and a natural culture, which is always solved by replacement, for the sole and greatest increase in oppression. The time has come for you to join me. Soon all the hostage sons will receive orders to return to Etzelburg."

A sentence sprung to Quixote's lips, and judging that his father had finished speaking, he blurted:

"But I'm in love with Rome's daughter!"

Attila laughed, not at the absurdity, as Quixote imagined, but the abruptness of his speech.

"Naturally."

Quixote did not reveal to Attila Rome's proposition. And during his stay a feverish succession of messages, numerous, many different and some repeated, arrived. All of this made him very uneasy.

"But how to preserve peace without trust?"

"Trust with hostages is not trust," Attila replied. "We are surrounded by enemies. But here, gathered in an expansive space, no one will come to dislodge us. We are too mobile and swift. Rome and Byzantium try to make me believe that they are using me to frighten each other. They have too many internal problems to make a move, yet, on the other hand, their structures are still strong enough to resist any fixed pressure I apply. The risk comes from the northern front, from the instability of the Germanic peoples. When we withdraw, we will have to do it in such a way that they do not descend in a chaos of dervishes to fill the vacuum. If not, the stability of the Empire could give way, and then it would be very difficult to escape the storm indeed."

These explanations did not quell Quixote's disquiet, but quite the opposite. "What does this mean? Attila's peace seems more dangerous than war, and this was the only thing I feared in coming . . ."

Weeks passed and one by one the hostages arrived from Rome and Constantinople. One day, Attila gave a banquet for the chiefs and their sons. In detail they recounted the Empire's situation: the state of its arts and letters, the state of its customs, the imperialization of religion, the peasant rebellions, political intrigues, and the army's mercantilism. Attila and Quixote listened in silence, but while Attila's thoughts ran through all these elements, Quixote did not think; he was only attentive to the elements themselves, passing from one to the other as if there were no interruption between them.

". . . and it's strange, there is currently no conflict between religions, Christianity respects paganism, or rather ignores it, but conflict powerfully permeates the sphere of philosophy. The real battle appears not to be waged in worship and belief, but in the organism and thought . . ." said one hostage.

". . . the Empire's borders are teeming with fresh Germanic mercenaries, warriors who for the most part have never seen a city . . ." said another.

According to custom, the guests departed all at once, just as they had arrived. Attila and Quixote were left alone.

"But Father, whether through war or peace, only we can prevent the material destruction of the classical world . . ." Quixote began, as if in response to something his father had already said.

Seated across from one another, Attila placed his right hand on Quixote's right knee, so that he sloped at the shoulders and did not meet his eye as he said: "The ruin will not just be material, and not all of the classical world will be ruined . . . only the imperatively classical. Ruin is the essence of the work, which mercilessly exposes what remains for what it is, a remainder, the completion that was only . . . and is now an ordained advance, in the rule and command sense." Attila stood now face to face with his son, so close that it hurt Quixote's eyes and he preferred seeing his father double. "Don't torture yourself. We are going to save this world . . . but not to save the salvageable but save the savior. We are going to build Nature, edify Nature . . . the classical was just the city. It won't be possible to say anymore that the classical 'is' the city, but rather the classical 'and' the city."

Quixote started, surprised and defensive, but swiftly smiled at Attila's complicit expression.

"But . . . even if we don't leave the world as it is, why not leave things as they are? Why not preserve them? Since the world of things is determined by subjects . . . why the need for . . ."

"What's made is not made once and for all but continues making . . ." Attila interrupted. "All the more perfect. For those things presented as perfect, remanence of advancement exerts an inexorable empire over the men who live with them. Or rather, in them. You cannot live 'with' a perfect thing, but 'in' a perfect thing. Open your eyes, the world as it is does not transcend things, even the most banally material and insignificant, it does not transcend things as they are." And thus they talked for much of the night, flanked by sentinels and horses sleeping on their feet.

While hunting in the Carpathians on the day the beaters raised a colossal boar, Attila and Quixote were riding through the densest part of the forest when both their mounts drew up short. They weren't as shocked by the sudden halt as by the almost premeditated nature of the simultaneity. They surrendered to this wise caprice of their steeds, and together their eyes turned upward, giving themselves over to the sojourn's shooting star, where light and shadow, interlaced in the foliage, lived without paying tribute to the day, and not one on the other's behalf, but one for the other. The earth seemed to have lost its gravity of attraction and was trying to retreat into its sentimental vanity, while the sky, the sky? Was decided that there half its dome was enough. The heads of the steeds looked like two carps in the water's glare.

"One can't reach the end except with everything," said Attila.

"Let's camp here and wait," said Quixote.

"If the absent makes progress, the present returns," Attila said.

"But even if it's not today, the present is here," Quixote said to Attila.

"No. Only tomorrow is here. And tomorrow has to go. Either that progress absents itself, or yesterday will not arrive at today."

Just then, having eluded the hunters and broken off the many arrows bristling from its flanks against the trees, the hideous boar came toward them, not at a run, but with steady steps. Neither the horses nor the riders flinched. The beast stopped between them.

"What loses us is what saves us."

"Yes," Attila replied. "But what loses us may perhaps be the most difficult of acknowledgments."

With his royal escort, the boulder of bristles and splinters emerged from the thicket.

Lying to port and starboard by six triremes in battery formation, the imperial bireme nodded tip to tail to the most secondary nature, like the temple of Janus always nods to the wind. The Roman fleet was returning from Africa, the expedition against the Vandals lost, by sea as well as by land. Carthage fell back, harbinger again, and now in the hands of a people who, having no art, desired history.

But what was that ominous episode to Rome? No sign of mourning tarnished the Valentinian house nor the Ostial jubilation, for Rome saw in itself not an imperial person, nor a repository of such persons, but the very essence of triumph, indifferent to victory.

The Numidian slave, a gift from Rome, withdrew under Ipsibidimidiata's approving gaze.

"That I should have returned from Africa to see you, do you not find it excessive?"

Ipsibidimidiata gathered up the folds of her stole from the biclinium and protested, but in supplication. "You know how uncomfortable I am in the Capitol."

"Where is Quixote?"

"He won't be long," replied Ipsibidimidiata, with an oily naturalness.

"Does he please himself here as much as you do?"

Laughing, one of the diners choked so seriously on an ortolan that, amid chuckles and wheezing, he severed all threads of the conversation. He left the table between two more-than-diligent servants, so apoplectically florid that it was as if they were escorting a plump blood sausage from the table.

"At first, I thought of entrusting Quixote with the report on the border defenses and the selection of hostages from the Empire . . ."

The feline 'S' of Ipsibidimidiata's back and neck accentuated its grace as she nodded, not at what she had just heard, but at what she expected to hear next.

". . . but then I considered that his magnificent erudition would be ill-used. The census of imperial art or the codification of law would do him more justice."

Ipsibidimidiata's eyes winked in time.

"Of course," continued Rome, "in that case, you would have to return . . ."

The prospect of returning to Rome did not disturb the splendid arc comprised of her lips and cheeks over the roundest teeth of that ivory treasure.

Nor did the autumn zephyr make the conjured image of Quixote flicker. An invisible rain sequined her skin, dotting it like a storm on a pond. She asked for a shawl.

The banquet had reached peak frenzy, and the clamor of conversations was beginning to wane. That was the chosen moment for Cretan and Egyptian dancers to burst in. To the sounds of cymbals and castanets, of the sistrum and tambourine, tightrope walkers and tumblers leaped, the acrobats flew, making a mosaic of interest while concentrating the amusement. The dancers followed, accompanied by the flute, lyre, or trumpet. The musician playing this last instrument moved to the back of the room, behind the triclinium, where Ipsibidimidiata had installed a hydraulic organ between two porphyry pillars. It was evident from the way he studied it that he was not curious but rather surprised to find it there and eager to play it. The dances finished, and Ipsibidimidiata gave instructions for the organist to be assisted. Plutonic music in the reflected vault of heaven filled the dining room. And yet there was something sea-like in that resonance, an echoing of wind through Neptune's caves. Everyone applauded, but without acclamations, as the enthusiasm began to subside. Strangely, the piece took on a simultaneously public dimension. Suspended in the atmosphere, it filled that contrast with tacit expectation. Bonifacio gave voice to the general request.

"Ipsibidimidiata, there is no one here who is unaware of your poetic gifts. Please, quench . . . quench our thirst for music."

Rome, too, had his pupils hooded by Mnemosyne, and Ipsibidimidiata truly did to please her father that night. She removed her cloak and took center stage on the triclinium. One of the musicians handed her the lyre.

> Just two rays the stars do have
> Because today they are crying,
> The moon that Mercury stole in Ostia
> Leaves on Pannonia cyclostomatic slime
> For Venus always has four rays
> Because she cries and drools while laughing.

There was a general guffaw, and Ipsibidimidiata looked at Bonifacio mockingly.

Again she plucked the strings.

The day does not allow the dawn to go,
The day does not allow the dusk to come,
And neither does the dawn finish coming out
Nor the dusk entering.

Why separate the daughter from the father?
Why separate the son from the mother?
And the sun rips the dawn from the sky,
And from the earth the dusk.

Reproach the day the bloody glow
Thank the night for twilight
If rejection of wakefulness is possible
Within the hope of sleep.

How will the earth be deflowered
If the sky is not illuminated?
Let the sun allow the sky to make life
So that the earth may make love.

Where is the night that follows the dawn,
The night that precedes the dusk?
Where is the sky born and loving,
The husband of the earth?

Poor virgin condemned to toil,
Repeating her daily forced labor!
Poor captive of the day,
Cinderella of hope!

Someone will have to open the horizons
To aid the exodus of the dawn,
To aid the entry of the angel
Who reveals the dusk.

Someone must unfold the night,
White, a day of all the stars,
Night of love in which the sun and the earth
Are two among them.

To the right, in the west, the Dolomites were diminished, for the freshly fallen snow, pure as a newborn's eyes, not only blended with the clouds but with the very blue of the sky and with their truncated peaks resembled volcanoes made young again, ready to rouge a perpetual sunset, or podiums, ready to receive the other titans, those who avoided Tartarus and positioned themselves above the cupola, judging the west to be more empyrean and the east more imperial. The waters of the Piave were experiencing their second year of the year, that which immediately precedes old age, in all that is alive and therefore cyclical, and its course, already well below Belluno's martial echoes, nonetheless looked like the bed of a lightning bolt, a mold forged by Vulcan, as if the humiliated god was reminding the cocksure one that there are no weapons without fire. Between the Postumia and Emilia roads, the sweetness of the plain clung to the rider's eyes, to the horses' hooves, the beauty of the future plain tiring them more than the expanse of the past plain. But riding along the Reno, the Apennine coolness soon dispelled that nostalgia.

The Cassian Way, a solid current, always favorable to the traveler no matter his direction, owed its privilege to the varied Etruscan charm, the motley dream of its valleys sleeping on the slope of mountains more sociable than associated, not a bit haughty, playing tic-tac-toe with the lakes. The cypresses, guardians of Etruria, marked that barmy distance, with a patience and gravity that were garnish and seasoning to the pleasant indolence of so much relieved irresponsibility. There everything was above everything, being under nothing, and Clusium, Volsinii, Veii, the happiest cities in Italy, looked caught between jumps, leaving a strange feeling of luck in the eyes, as if instantaneously before or after there was nothing else there but one of those mountainsides, frolicking like pups with the wind or with shadow.

He reached the Tiber via the Flaminian Way, and leaving the latter followed the former to circle 'round Rome. The belly of Hadrian's Mausoleum, antimother threatening to birth the Aelian Bridge and the city inside, slowed the river there even more than the bend, and the shadow it cast over the rider and the mount was less absence of light than presence of tar, impermeable even to the commotion coming from the Naumachia Circus.

It looked as if Ostia had washed meat in the sea, and the sun didn't want to sink, squashing down from top to bottom to become nautical and sail across the horizon to another element more worthy of immersing itself. As for the horse, it stopped, hesitating, but Quixote didn't give it time to act on its desire to continue southward, and they entered the city.

———

Without the slightest intention, it was the total unawareness of being clothed that stripped them naked. They didn't leave their clothes, but rather their clothes entered that cast-off world we call, granting them no small measure of vitality, objects. And so, not yet touching each other, in another sifting world they held each other through their eyes, and even felt the edge of a fingernail and the end of a strand of hair as communally their own. An anguish that seemed not infinite but innate, not that it would never end but that it had never begun, that it was the sudden intensification of a latent anguish hitherto only intuited, an anguish that promises to end giving difficult but unique access to a breadth, itself infinite and innate, so perfectly new that time fit inside without being second and nonetheless unscrewed. It seemed they weren't surprised by this novelty but rather that they remembered it, somewhat like one remembers a promise once it's fulfilled, only here the promise had never been distinctly formulated, and this fulfillment was much more novel than the mere perfection of what it announced. It seemed too that everyone saw them, that the whole world was present, and they felt neither shame nor embarrassment, nor was it felt on their behalf, and they witnessed the scene, themselves children, and not multiplied in their prior ages but singular, yet the whole past was unfolding, syncytial personages of today expanded in an implosion of yesterday. And the walls, to speak of what was most immovable, solid and permanent in their immediate environs, not only eschewed the function of opacity but neither supported, covered, or sheltered, they in fact performed no function at all except that of a simple dramatic backdrop, otherwise completely fortuitous and gratuitous, interchangeable with something else, or better yet, nothing. Things appeared before them, and the mystery of all apparent leaped to their senses, the intense mystery of extensive appearance, the metaphysics of profound continuity, the fair unfolding of its complexity. The appearance of the superficial, floating like a lotus, but from memory, the love that enveloped and penetrated poetry, the formal creativity, the shapes present in that moment. This breadth, however, exceeded its fullness, and the emptiness of that excess promised more novelty than its full flaw, and, overall, the present enthusiasm was accompanied less by an exaggerated appreciation than by a pusillanimous one, giving siphoned way to a reversal felt futuristically toward an anguish of another kind, more intense and inclined than the other. This notwithstanding, the pure (for being present) value of the previously appreciable, the pure (for being present) quality of the previously measurable, and (for being passive) mensural, since everything, that is, every one of the things (and for being mutually presented, all), were actors, unstable and dense, antimonial and leaden, in that insistent affirmation of a solid beat, no intervals in the frequency, not like a liquid rhythm, and especially not like a gaseous rhythm, both of which only exist negatively, by virtue of the non-being of their measured hiatuses. Yes, they felt, what a marvelous tangency between consciousness and solidity, a herald of the penetration between consciousness and solidity that, in that contact, relegated from a distance the supposed preeminence of the liquid, gaseous, igneous, and ethereal. What a marvel of immediacy between the conscious soul and solid death. They looked in each other's eyes, and as if through the rays of their mutually starry images, they saw each thing as never before, with double belonging. Yes, that's it. They held each other in their gazes, and gradually, things began to be held in their gazes, in comical weightlessness. The bodies of the earth are the shadows of the spirit deposited by the bodies of the heavens, and only in heaven can a facet with two focal points fit, two points of view and one dimension.

"Would not 'subviving' be the correct term?" Quixote dreamed, and awoke. Ipsibidimidiata was no longer resting upon him, and immediately he looked for her. Seated on a besellium, brushing her hair, she looked out the window. Seated in a corner of a besellium, with the foreshortened view of her profile, the part showing forehead and cheekbone and chin but hiding eye and nose and mouth, streaked by her spilling hair, finer as the combing progressed, she watched the night kneeling in her own lap, the night eating her hands, which, for being so full, could not come together and pray, full of the limits they had endured during the day, during themselves, and almost everyone had suffered, for almost everyone are themselves, are perfect, and how few things remained nocturnal by day, hands full of that very thing which empties them, nocturnal night unto itself, devoured by things, seized by the day of things, upon which the memory of the day of things parasitically lives, covered in blisters full of those memories, drowning those memories of itself, emaciated hands of the night full of those blisters, how were they to pray? "Yes, 'subviving' must be the correct term," thought Quixote, and stood.

He approached her without stealth, entrusting instinct with the necessary noise to alert her to his approach without diverting her attention, but rather including himself in her sphere while simultaneously expanding it with his own, refractive, in a joint attention that was refracted yet not hybrid. He placed his hands on her shoulders, round, firm, and soft as a dove's breast, and the night came to be understood in what they knew, that the skin is the loupe of the eye and ear, and to the double loupe of their skins the night came to understand, bringing the close closer by magnification and pushing the far farther away by inversion, discontinuing the distance, sinking the sagittal depths into its midst, losing all notion of range, of parabola, of symbol, and to that acoustic loupe came the night's murmured, muffled sounds, embalming love and survival. He leaned his forehead against her head and she felt how her occiput shaped his face, and her sense of self was personified in him more than in herself, and he felt his face shielded by her occiput, and that his sense was personated less in it than in his own, and both gained a sense of being, of self, certainly, but even more so of consciousness. They were more conscious, and the best part of that expansion was that they were on the edge, not feudalizing the senses from the cranium but conversely, like in poetry, and it seemed that their senses were in direct communication, and that even their organic identities were set aside to allow for this revolution that, for the first time, did not distill the origin, did not filter it, but distilled, refined, and perfected the end. And so creation did not recreate by recreating itself but by re-expanding, for all that not only concerned the two of them and the five senses we call relational, but also all the hitherto subconscious senses and vegetative senses, and even unsuspected senses, how else to explain that, within them, even the mineral had consciousness, that the penetration of the three realms would not expand until their inclusion but that they would conclude, in a circulation of sense that was not empathy or mere panphilia but the maximum arches of the orb of the three elements, the empyrean orb of the three stable elements, arches of the maximum circles of the halo of the three pulses, the amorphous, the essential, the archaic beating of the earth, the adult beating of the water, formal, classic, which always rises toward the sky, the young beating of the air, the metamorphic, which always descends toward the earth. And they heard in themselves the rhythm of the two rhythms of the Ostian beach, the rhythm of water, best heard in dead calm, and the rhythm of air, best heard in a swell. And between them they understood the compound world, a complexity of elements, by the rhythms of the folds. The complex world was caught, hung on each reflection, by the rhythms of those folds. And it was unnecessary to un-fold the night's arcana, the night's archaic youth, the night's youthful maturity, which is young maturity because youth is archaic, its youth is archaic so that its maturity is young. In truth the time of day was nothing more than one shore of night's time, a byway of night's path, and the day was just a wake in the nocturnal sea.

Ipsibidimidiata woke first this time. Quixote's arm lay across her chest, its weight reassuring, or rather it didn't weigh at all, it was contained archimedically in her body, as if the title page of a poem in folios were its paperweight. Ipsibidimidiata caressed the arm, and it didn't seem like one of her own, rather that upon her hand she felt what the arm and the skin under the arm felt. Her fingers were multiplied by the well-traveled touch of soft vellus. The night had played so rowdily with Quixote's figure that now, asleep on his side, his one visible eye didn't appear to sit on his cheekbone but on the edge of his nose, like a ctenophore poised to dive to the bottom of the abyss. Remaining on her back, Ipsibidimidiata turned her head and looked out the window. The fine and luminous reticulum of the night had disappeared in the east, without the dawn having produced the slightest dilution, blur, or scratch on the intense darkness. She knew that soon it, too, would disappear in the west, and that the web would unravel, quickly, toward the dome, toward the compluvium of that dome through which neither water nor light entered but from which night and fire would emerge. And despite the morning star's cherubic dissuasion, soon there would be no deep midnight but only broad half-night before the metallic precursors of dawn.

"Darling!"

Quixote's breath changed rhythms and he snuggled against her.

"Where does the night go from one day to the next?"

It wasn't a question but a complaint, which was echoed in Quixote's silence. They pressed closer to one another, squashing their faces together until they felt teeth through their lips and eyes through their lids. They stayed that way . . .

Then they got up. They drank some water.

Without preamble: "What did your father want?"

"Attila wants me to return to Etzelburg for good . . . All the hostages of the Empire are being summoned. He wants us to return to the heart of Asia, where we will gather the hostages from all the Empires. Then he will abandon Rome to the Visigoths and Ostrogoths, China to the Mongols, and India to the White Huns. His . . ."

"And what is my place in that roving desire?" Ipsibidim-idiata huffed.

"He knows we love each other. I even think he has known it for a long time. And I would say it pleases him, that it even fulfills one of the yearnings of his providential character so typical . . . He said nothing explicitly, but it was abundantly clear that he expected you to come with me. That he was waiting for both of us."

"Is he in a hurry?"

"I think so. Although he wouldn't call it hurry. One must avoid delay to avoid getting ahead of oneself, that's his idea of diligence. When the day arrives, there's no room in it for hours, nor minutes in the hour, nor seconds in the minute. And once things are underway, nothing and no one will stop it, and only those who join it will recapitulate its arrival."

"Rome is also in a rush," Ipsibidimidiata continued. "A rush for us to live in Rome." For all the hostages to hold positions of responsibility in the Empire, and you the greatest among them. To reorganize the border defenses and consolidate political consciousness . . . He is counting on us, and in Rome's accounting there is no division or subtraction . . ."

From the dawn, a blister on the Latin horizon, the sun sprouted green, a cold nail on the blushless blister, unhealthy wound that had not bled, itself light's cauterization of an earth sieved through metal without being cleansed. Contrasting with that violence, that onslaught, the night, detached from the earth on all horizons, serenely retreated from the sky, truth be told, a balm for the eyes, frugality that didn't seem to border the light directly, that seeemed to veil itself in situ, the absence of night veiled with the absence of light, in a celestial no-man's land.

It was then that . . . but wait, where were they coming from? . . . the thistle seeds appeared, floating in the southern wind . . . not that they appeared arriving but that they appeared being on the southern wind that blew, which had been blowing all night, gently without gusts or breaks, constant, unchanged, and close to the ground . . . legions of unshakeable thistle seeds tumbling through the air, conveying a loose, leisurely movement . . . alighting . . . landing . . . taking off again. The air had a spectral frost, imbued with the saturnine season, the chrysanthemum flock, a shepherd king, who endorses gold in order to draw purple to his breast, the Arcadian king of a migrating sky, flock of stars landing among a flock of kings, the nocturnal chrysanthemums in their manure-dipped boots, dictating laws of love, from autumn to spring, unwitting lovers of peonies, a love assembled without clockworks, interlocked beyond the stoppage and spring, not committed, pledged, captivated, which did not redeem the flaw of its origin but the flaw of its end ... precession of waking in sleep, thistle seed and chrysanthemum, enigma-less visitation.

". . . that phobia of the city as if it were a vice of history . . . reservoir of history that stagnates its energy and corrupts its best hope . . . that hatred of the wall, the roof, and political volume . . . of cubic reason . . . that lack of trust in the urban economy, monetary economics . . . in the radial administration of the law . . . all of that has led him to cultivate a strange project, according to which civilization can only continue to develop by destroying the city . . . as if it were possible to speculate in philosophy without speculating in trade . . . as if both were not specifically political, condemned to be produced simultaneously in the same crucible of interests . . . he doesn't see that the leisure of poetry is not possible without the business of slavery . . . and that if the proportional and condensed imitation of Nature leads to imitable art par excellence, then those same qualities lead to the amphitheater's inimitable spectacle . . . He wants to change the river's course . . . but how to change the course without interrupting it? and how to interrupt a course without losing all flow? . . . Who dares to think . . . to destroy all the world's cities . . . in the name of an orbicular civilization . . ."

"Now I see," Ipsibidimidiata interrupted, "that your father and mine aren't enemies but something much worse and more insurmountable . . . and that if their Horai were to guard the gates of Mount Olympus, every meeting of the gods would be alienated . . . for they couldn't recognize each other . . . face to face they would always find themselves on a precipice, and in profile on an apex . . . they truly live reciprocally in another space, in another orbit, in another movement and idea . . . irreducible to the sphere. For Rome considers himself an eagle-like phoenix, and will employ all his forces to balance himself westward, to gather, to resurge as a republic, to absorb the new adjacent alienation into his power . . . justifying its oppression with the community of glory, identifying the world with his epic, and more and more intensely and exclusively with his epic, ultimately tolerating drama as an illustration, and the lyre as a play of the senses . . ."

"Your father half-dead, and mine half-mad . . . and in its half-madness Attila's civilizing idea does not die . . . and for being half-dead Rome's idea of civilization does not go mad . . . and one for the other: one without the other . . ." Quixote interrupted.

"What do you mean?"

"That neither Attila nor Rome matter, neither the Huns nor the Romans, just the city, palatial, Olympian, dominant over any other order, whether natural or human. What matters is not a Rome bequeathed to culture or a Roman Rome . . . but their confluence, for the sole good of the city . . . the confluence of the steppe and the forum, if it benefits the city . . . for Roman is not a gentilic, and to be Roman isn't to be native to Rome, rather it is the city and not its inhabitants, the city itself, present, and not the genealogy of its population that grants autochthony . . . Since Hadrian, the idea of a Roman Rome is anachronistic—progressively and irrevocably. Rome and Attila are outside of history . . . one immobilizing himself in his atavism, the other dissolving from his own . . . but together . . . Hunnic Rome . . . dissolving that immobility, fusing Hunnic atavism into the mold of penetration, into the idea of the bore hole of the city . . . For just as life is invaginated into its species in order to be reproduced and evaginates into others in order to be preserved . . . so history invaginates in the city and evaginates in the vanquished . . . the migrant subjects . . . and there is no other way of being in history, just as there is no other way of being alive . . . Only invasion can save the city, only Attila can save Rome . . ."

"But that's precisely what neither one wants!" Ipsibidimidiata interjected.

"I know . . . I know . . . And to make it worse, as you've said and is true, not only are your father and mine strangers to each other, but I am an enemy to both because of my idea . . ."

"You know?" Ipsibidimidiata interrupted, "the thunder is among the leaves . . . base and axis . . . base and axis . . . between the rhythm of water and the rhythm of air . . . between the difference of space and differential space . . . The air rows on the eagle and the water rows on the dove . . . the earth on the butterfly . . . and you and I . . . and you . . . and us . . . We fit . . ."

Quixote embraced her. "We fit."

Through the window he saw that the freedman had drawn six buckets of water from the well. That's how long the storm had lasted. Unusual for this time of year, it seemed to have taken much longer, breaking up time in the subjects, leaving the impression of uncomfortable settling in, of a broken now that respected the place of objects. The Assyrian mastiff rose, moved to the other side of the room, turned a half dozen times around its tail, sniffing the ground, decided not to lie down, and returned to where he started from.

"What's all that to us?" Quixote said, not loosening his arm. "In the end, it's fortunate that they are both outside of history, and I won't be the one to provoke them! Let us avoid it ourselves, as well. Our love is more important than the city. Let us alienate history in our poetry, while they continue alienating it in their ideas . . ."

". . . While . . . how long will that while last?"

"Nobody can answer that. We aren't the only protagonists; other peoples want to enter history, and each holds the master key to the city . . . that while doesn't depend solely on us, on Attila and Rome . . . there are other peoples, hungry and thirsty for history, deified by revenge, original by divine right, fertile by origin, irresistibly attracted, sucked in by the virtual void of the city, the absence of Rome from the city . . . a void more abhorred by the city than by Nature, incomparably, medium, environment, element, circumstance, and instance, of re pe ti tion . . . do you understand? perfect, the perfect sphere, every tail as tip." Beads of sweat crowned Quixote's brow.

Ipsibidimidiata ran her thumbs over them and planted a kiss on his forehead. She smiled, relaxed, grateful, and a little defensive . . . Quixote's laughter was lacking in vowels.

"I bet you already know which of the requests we'll entertain."

"Of course I do! And you already know, my little trickster, that I have nothing left to bet you . . ."

Ipsibidimidiata shrugged one shoulder and set her other hand on her hip.

Quixote smiled and his eyes looked like two mouths. "Better to pretend to be deaf. Your father doesn't have Attila's patience. That's an Asian virtue, reserved for those who know what a horizon is, where sky and earth intertwine. What European nation knows that? Impatient, all of them, impatient to not change and to change, always impatient . . . that's where the danger lies. So I'll make the one who can bear to wait, wait . . ."

"But you told me he was in a hurry?"

"My absence won't delay his plan, that's all I meant. Asian punctuality never implies violence. But if I could convince Rome to give me a role in the building of the border defenses . . . well, that's what it all depends on in the end! That if Rome is able . . ."

But neither Quixote said what he was talking nor did Ipsibidimidiata hear what he said next . . . "to be contained within geographic borders and secure constructions . . ." increasingly muffled . . . because they were there and the night was enveloping the sun, like orbital bone and eyelids envelope the eye, like mouth and lips envelope the tongue, like essence envelops being, like allegory envelops symbol . . . they themselves were an extension, a pointillist projection of the night's essence, enveloping the being of day, the sphere

. . . the sphericity of light . . . sphericity being, not essential but being . . . but they themselves not mere concavity in the containment of the sphere of day, but convexity too, bodies, presences in another space, in the bosom of a cone, close in the deepest reaches, coiled not from where the infinitude of the expansion, capable of containing all sphericity, could be perceived, but to where the cone, born on the other side of the point, could be sensed, the sphereless space on the other side of the vertex . . . there they were, occluding the day with a kiss, blind not from enucleation but from concentration, mute from being imprinted and not from losing their tongues.

It wasn't a dream, but somehow she realized while asleep that she was alone. This woke her, and without wasting a second on confirming whether or not Quixote was in bed, she got up from the side by the window. The moon, elliptical from top to bottom, appeared to simultaneously wax and wane, like an egg, which, having reached a state of perfection, should want to make itself perfectible, never new again . . . and clapper not sounding but sonant thanks to the bell's collapse. Then she saw Quixote, under the moon, who seemed to be walking on a rolling pin, among the oleanders, no, among the carob trees, and noticed for the first time that the rhythm of his legs, and of his arms! was none other than the rhythm of water, and likewise the slight nod of his head, vegetal rhythm par excellence . . . how was that?, and as if evoked without citation, Lucretius appeared . . . 'why is De rerum natura written backward . . . why does it start with the beginning of the end and then continue right on, without a change to its meaning, to the end of the beginning . . . as if the nature of things walked backward in things, repeating death, and not birth although it believes and wants to, contradicting . . . the strength of things, splitting them in the past tense, separating them in the wake, reducing them in the golden mirage of age, dividing them into cause and the applicable nostalgia? . . . poor things, increasingly caused . . . poor cause, each thing increasingly vicarious . . . and decreasingly vicissitudinous . . . poor occasion, each cause plurally fantastic, and its thing singularly immaterial."

Woe to the drama if unexpected actors enter the stage, spontaneous maskless individuals and troupes with tongue. For the masks are limited and they will have to successively grab them in order for everyone to appear, and the piece will be confused. Woe to the drama if a spectator enters the stage, for he will make an amphitheater of the theater. Woe if geography enters history. For someone will lose their point of view and will not spot hope at the bottom of Pandora's box.

One morning, marl and amber encountered the Gepids on their doorsteps. Parting gifts. The brined cattle were already heading inland, and not only did the dogs make no attempt to stop them, but covered their flanks, trotting in the manner in which one quarter is always at rest, following an order unexpected only to the commanders because they had to apply it themselves. The cattle followed the oldest bullock, the dogs followed the cattle, and man followed the dog, leaving a sea no longer blue or gray but intensely green to the fish that knew neither how to graze its bottom nor the expired responsibilities in suspension.

The old bullock persisted in his inherited post, the original pact between his Moor and the grass, between his snout and the blade, instinct imprinted on each one of his cells and more deeply expressed for being nearer extinction, a model that preceded him like a herd of innumerable bullocks, infinitely more numerous than the heads of cattle following him. And so herbivores, carnivores, and animivores followed that fatuous fire of grass, ghost-generator of meat, ghost-generator of soul.

A clay mosaic. Illustrating that liquid is a divided solid. Water had permitted such a revelation of its essence. As if the extreme aridity called the solid to be liquid for something else. And just as the water was liquid for the sand, now the sand was liquid for the clay, demonstrating the desert's marine structure, and in doing so flaunting the desert structure of the sun. But that clay mosaic, why had it been liquid? To inlay the reversibility of the sun and the sky? How to inlay the finger of a glove? No, that clay inlay was the liquid for the Moor, demonstrating the nomadic structure of necessity, and thus flaunting the sedentary nature of greed.

Silhouettes on the dune slope, the dromedaries reflected various associations, or rather, clarified associated variables, the symbiosis between the palm tree and the spring, the disconcertion of the apes in its fronds, each confused, not by a dateless paradise, but by a cage without accessories, the spooning of the pacing and the unscrewing of the haze, which disrupted the hypotenuse on the horizon, the boundaries receding in stages, so that a stumble in the air was required to avoid stepping on the sudden Caesarian and proconsul cities.

Meanwhile, from the forests of Germania, crowds of children emerged, haloing adolescents who in turn went 'round the adults, the most aged at the center, like oil stains spreading in water, the peripheries, being less dense, reflecting the tenderest colors, they emerged from the forest's southern edge, through trunks as black as the pilings on a cluster of stilt houses, bathed in a lake of dark air, containing liquid rooms at bird's eye view and solid rooms at snake-height, whence all those cross-bearing children had come, themselves the flying-kites of other children who entered the forest from the northern edge and were born without navels, and between all of some of them and all the others there was but a single string, which the adults endeavored to grab hold of, and which the most aged and the adolescents endeavored to release, the latter with expressions of impatience and the former with expressions of horror.

Rain bows over hermetic wave, braided sky over furrowed sea, the coiffure suspended the hair, and the hair suspended the face, formed by the eyes, fishers of pearls, invaginated by the wave, fishers of pearls fished by pearls, a vicious circle when both were seen together from behind, distant, in their rostral form, more strabismic when viewed individually, one separately recalling the other, but neither convergent nor divergent, but only and as much, alone as much as revergent: for as the braid of sky crossed over the furrow of the sea, its branches inverted, or perhaps, or rather, or surely, it was that inversion of the branches that furrowed the sea, it was that point of the rainbow's spectral transmutation that canceled the wave, not by opening a passing furrow, but by obliterating a fold that was, and the face suspended the body, all of it like the night suspends the flame and the flame suspends the candle by the wick, thus the light spread through its cleavage, lucidly losing itself through its body, and the body was nothing except its own face but hidden.

There, on the threshold, the space in the room appeared to stall . . . and the hall to time her transit. When she set off walking, that sense stayed with her, and both men felt less restriction and rush. They were seated almost facing each other, between the main threshold of the room and the window. Ipsibidimidiata came to her father first, kissed him, and then went to sit beside Quixote, without passing between them. Though she didn't seek it, just as if it was the end of the arm of the chair, her hand came to rest naturally on Quixote's.

"Forgive me if I have interrupted you."

"No, you've arrived just in time, after the preambles, which is typical of you," Rome said, "and neither I nor Quixote," and Quixote smiled, nodding at Rome's glance with a smile, "could hope for a better intermission than for you to appear. But I will stop you before you begin, as I see in your eyes that you have many things to recount, go on, your whole morning . . ." Ipsibidimidiata cocked her head slightly toward one shoulder and began to laugh in protest, "and the only time I have left today is subject to the Empire. Here is what I wanted to tell you: Quixote, I entrust you with the census of pretorian decrees and edicts for the new constitution of civil law. Present yourself tomorrow in Trajan's Forum," and seamlessly turned to Ipsibidimidiata with a look he knew to be ever the more tender for being more authoritarian and vice versa, telling her: "and you, now that isn't what you've been up to this morning," and Ipsibidimidiata and Quixote's fingers found one another, "you know what you must do next: find the villa you like most . . . look for the least Roman," and he winked, but the gesture missed Ipsibidimidiata and passed between the two lovers.

Rome uncrossed his legs and they unclasped their hands, ready to stand when Rome stood. But he did not, he only held out both arms. Quixote was the first to reach him and presented him with his right hand made into a fist, which Rome enveloped in his own, shaking it, but when Ipsibidimidiata reached his side, he grabbed her by the wrist, barely squeezing. Before they responded with a new gesture to all of that, Rome rose to his feet, brought his hands together and released them with a light push toward them both, between them both, still holding hands, their projection led them straight to the main door to the hall. In this way, with a naturalness that undid the art of discretion and reverence while maintaining the ambivalence of authority, they parted.

Rome had not been mistaken. Once Quixote's role in the city was made firm, Ipsibidimidiata beat the capital to flush out the least Roman house. Excluding both the administrative and most populous neighborhoods from the start, she soon decided her preference for suburban residential areas over those within the city, and thus, in just a few days, moved from the Palatine to her new house which was near the Porta Nomentana and so like the house in Ostia, owing more to its furnishings, brought from the old Valentinian house to the Capitol, than its façades, terraces, and gardens, all south and west facing as well, only here cypresses and olive trees were more abundant than mimosas and oleanders, and the scents did not blend but neither did they endure, and in contrast the sounds blended and the noise endured. Or, as all the citizens knew without knowing how to say it, without even knowing how to think it or feel what they knew, soundlessly the duration sounded.

For the city endured because of a secret compromise between the Capitol and the suburbs, the submerged part of the city that spilled over underground, a secret compromise that attractively affected its subcelestial opposites, its singulars, and for those who did not escape the least Roman house and the Palatine, filling the streets and squares one by one, the space between the spokes of the wheel and between the ground and the lifted sole, the secret mission held in common and the secret transmitted by appropriation that endured between the common grave and the pantheon, the wake's epithalamic compromise, the noise, in sum, with which all things premature endure, dirt in the air, water in the fire, splitting off the halo, promise split from hope, promise and hope committed like the afterglow of the sun and afterglow of the moon, inventing a memory of love, inventing it until it bursts forth almost in dreams, in the prevention of mourning, for the village cotillion, the whole village with no milestones on the road nor any communal boundary markers, whose remnant of the halo was the city, novelty in opposition to fullness, novelty foreseen with a spyglass, imminence resulting from the double's crime because of the insulted imminence of the half, beauty of the ossifrage city, mortgaged to its foundations, determined down to the humblest antefix to make flesh with its bones, an atavistic great-great-great-grandson, fornicating in the cupolas, the resonance of noise not the echo of sound, inducing more origin than Nature, which did not illuminate it like this, made sick on it, growing but armed in the womb, in the scar of the womb, in the cyst of the scar, and resonating solid in the liquid, resonating liquidly solid in the cacophony of the unborn rhythms, from the segments of the halo navigators in the osmazome of religious affairs, beings of Nature, flagrant analogism between composition and synthesis, wandering in the visceral void, virtueless void, deserted by the water, by the rhythms, at the beginning of air, novice of air, falsified learner, proclaiming on every Roman corner, vocatively, vacuously, the commitment between the airy earth and the burning water, of the earth and the air in the water and the fire, segments pulsing nonetheless, segments of halo nonetheless beating out a rhythm but without reciprocal preposition, nucleus of the earth wishing it were crust, from the inalienable rhythm of the earth, beating in the cemeteries and the wedding bed, pit of the rhythm of the earth wishing it were its pulp, almond of the rhythm of the earth wishing it were its shell.

Sacrifice of the animal on the horizon and the vertical sacrifice of the man engaged in the buried dirt and discharged water. Empyrean and Hell engaged in the final judgment: in the children of essence.

That night, Rome saw just one star in the heavens, a dot, neither original nor final, a period beyond the sentence, with no direction or meaning, indeclinable. But the star, the annual ray of the star, only reflected on Rome a terrapin, a dolorous terrapin, in all the adjective's ambivalence, neither transfixed nor affixed, but transfixing and asphyxiating, dolorous for the star and pained for the moon, the absent one, understood, as it were, to be the star.

What the annual ray did not see was that on the southern edge of the Black Forest, the kites were turning somersaults.

". . . that story of redemption . . . It's God's redemption . . . not the redemption of humanity," Quixote was thinking as simultaneously Luculus—the Historian converted, recycled, into Legislator—said to himself, "Poor wretch," considering the poet he saw in Quixote ". . . aboard the very same galley . . ."

But the critical accounting of the pretorian failures in the Dacia, lost and unredeemed, not only lingered in those lapses of interest on the part of the bureaucrats but stumbled into an entire office paralyzed by the verified intelligence: "Strasbourg has fallen!"

All present looked at one another, even the most myopic sought out another pair of eyes, and Quixote's found those of Luculus, and this man knew that that man understood what had made him think the sentence that had trotted through his head when the news erupted, the thing that was now dawning on them all, in the hypermetropic parallelograms they comprised, seeing out the eyes that were watching them . . . and the facts were soon confirmed . . . for it was crystal clear that Rome, the Dacian gold lost, the Hispanic metals uncertain, could not be willing to abandon the silver to the Burgundians, and that in order to recover it and preserve the strategic Raetia, it would have to halt its defensive policy and, in the absence of a large campaign that for the time being seemed both expensive and premature, unleash a series of punitive expeditions one after another in an intensifying ramming strategy sent to contain the Burgundians and force their retreat without the intention to destroy or suppress them. What caused the forensic examiners the most anguish regarding what they understood was the irrevocable precedent that would result from that reaction from Rome, not whether or not it was a success or a failure, but that it was untimely.

Rome's military operations were victorious but the triumph was pyrrhic. Rome's triumph, for the first and last time, despite subsequent victories and defeats, was pyrrhic. For in dislodging the wolf without managing to cut off access to the bear, the Germans occupied the void left by the Burgundians, who did not billet themselves where Rome had prepared but, obeying motives that had nothing to do with push received in the Roman attack, did not retreat but rather advanced eastward, unleashing in a counterwave the complex floating port extending between the Rhine and Danube basins, a variable-ratio between an extemporaneous motive and placeless reason that disrupted the Empire's border defenses' capacity for anticipation.

If that weren't enough, and as if the most centripetal segments of a spiral compromised the most centrifugal segments of another combined spiral, the Vandals, surging from Constantinople, maritimely blocked the Italic peninsula and closed off the Adriatic Sea.

Hidden in a mosaic of swamps and pine forests, "if it weren't for the pines Ravenna would be Greek, if it weren't for the mire Ravenna would be Barbarian" went the song, the painted terrapin, partenogenetic miniature, not even italic, the daughter of Rome and mother of Constantinople, detached from both, senescent for both, detached from almost everything, Ravenna attended the pact, and its unnatural westernism. Constantinople would break the Vandal blockade and Rome was obliged to restore order on the continent.

As if one of the Ionic columns had sat down to talk with Ipsibidimidiata ... that strange vision was what Quixote had on returning home. It was the minister Onegesius, Attila's confidant. His enormous curls had the stubbornness of a ram and ivy's prehensile flexibility, evoking the gray eminence his smooth Ephesian forehead could not betray. Even from a distance, once he was recognized, his identity was clear. Onegesius himself in the imperial city! This was the second surprise, less striking than the first, but more penetrating. They were chatting amiably, with the unique easiness between friends who are discussing a serious matter, hammered out hundreds of times. Sensing the man's proximity, they both gave him a smile, as if they were about to go right back to their conversation . . . and yet they did not . . . or as if they were about to include him, acknowledged by him as well . . . but that wasn't it either, since instead they came to a full stop that surprised no one.

"At the head of the tribes of Mundzuk, Turda, Escemen, Eteo, Opos, Cadicha, Berendo, Sultan, Bulchu, Bolug, Zambur, Zamur, Reelo, Levente, Kulch, Ompud, Misk, Mik, and half of his own tribe, Attila is presently advancing at a steady march through the steppes of Asia, having discreetly made a gradual withdrawal from the Danubian scene . . . He heads east, to pull out in the same way and passing his people situated on the shores of the Aral Sea and Lake Baikal, since the barbarians of the great civilized empires of Asia are stomping, just as impatiently as here, gathering in nebulous pairs of war and destruction. He will rescue his hostages without them being cut in the downward spiral and, folding them into his people, he will rescue them without them being cut in the massacre . . . He will synchronize his grand plans, setting the date one day before history." Onegesius rose to his feet, and faced Quixote's profile, whose frontality, which converged with that of Ipsibidimidiata though they weren't looking at one another, at a point not synchronous but synesthetic only, immersed in their flotation, oscillating . . . "Attila has entrusted me personally," he bent his head slightly "to entrust you with the withdrawal of the rest of his people." Quixote stood, but his gaze still clung to the same spot . . . "He has specified that, given the small contingent, you are to do it with dazzling speed . . . In fact, the most recent events confirm his prudent foresight. For you must know that we have sustained an attack as fierce as it was unexpected from the Burgundians, whom we have annihilated near Etzelburg. Graver still, the Byzantines, breaking the pact of Ravenna, not only have not . . ."

Quixote's memory retained the words Onegesius spoke next, but his attention was on the point, no longer oscillating, from which it appeared an image wanted to be born, attaching to a cracked mirror . . . no, wanting to detach a whole mirror from a cracked image . . . "The conflict between the ignored and the . . . and the . . ."

"You won't find it . . . you won't find it . . ." Ipsibidimidiata's thought seemed to reach him.

". . . anchors raised, but the columns of their armies are rising through Thrace, with the deliberate aim of pushing us westward, not so much to cut off our retreat to the steppe, for they hardly intend to engage us in battle, but to use us as a propeller at the center of Europe, at its strategic heart, between Raetia and Italy . . ."

". . . The circumflexion between the broken and the . . . the . . ."

". . . You won't find it . . . there are as many missing words as excess ones, and all the words you know are excess . . ."

"Attila awaits you on the steppe to the north of the Altai, at the head of the other half of his own tribe and the tribes of Astur, Cham, Chus, Nembrod, Bor, Dama, Kelad, Keveo, Kear, Beler, Radar, Otmar, Tarkans, Bondoforte, Bukem, Chanad, Rudli, and Bezter."

In enduring those words, Quixote recalled only that Onegesius exited through a corner of the peristyle, blending in with the columns that seemed to follow him like a formation of crowned storks.

Perhaps it was a shooting star that had once been a comet, but was no longer. The sky was streaked. The magnificent black polyhedron which shone only at its infinitesimal limits with the sphere, was streaked . . . A white line, matte, clear, in one stroke. Not a flourish, but rather the printed dash on which something is to be written. A line that lacked the thickness of a beginning or the contour of an end . . . that seemed to come from its center . . . what center? . . . from that dot . . . what distinguished that dot from the others? . . . a star was missing . . . a star was missing! It had shifted, no, it had been scratched out, no, it had extinguished itself in its shifting . . . extinguished . . . ? Because that line was truly printed, engraved, and its edges scratched the cornea more than tangentially, more than an eye's touch . . .

Comploring . . . not compluviating . . . the lamenting of those two lovers . . . the . . . roof of their heartbreak removed.

"Rome sends me to Aetius as a military advisor against the Germans. I cannot accept. The reigning situation there is so confusing that the risk of war with the Huns is incalculable. And this despite Onegesius not yielding to Byzantine pressure. What treachery from Constantinople! Aware of Attila's absence, taking advantage of the Vandal blockade, it stokes conflagration on the Western continent, and hopes to behead the victor who has been bled dry in reconquering the entirety of the empire. How arrogant! Even if Attila and all the peoples who seek shelter beneath his idea retreat to the steppe, there and everywhere are sufficient forces to completely destroy Mediterranean civilization. And if, by chance, such a ruse were to succeed, what would become of classical civilization? What does that decadent youngster intend? . . . But neither can I accept Attila's command . . . I don't believe in his idea of an apolitical civilization . . . And executing our withdrawal condemns Rome to death. How to abandon . . . the excellent order of the abscissa of the seven hills . . . for that . . . the tempestuous disorder . . . of hills with no abscissa."

After Quixote's tormented consideration, a moment went by and a moment went on, yes, two moments, without an identifiable hiatus, before Ipsibidimidiata spoke, in this way both lovers lived that interval.

"Remember the rhetoric. Every dilemma is an incomplete reading that has a third alternative."

"Attila or Rome? Aborting a utopia is worse than tragedy triumphing."

"You cannot stay here. You have orders from Rome to join Aetius . . . our love, Quixote . . . let us save our love . . . you, me, and poetry, let us save our love story . . ."

"Yes, that is the complete reading: let us save ourselves . . ."

"Inland, beyond the western border of the Cyrenaica, there exists a Greek colony unredeemed by either empire. Some relatives of my mother live there."

Quixote breathed in Ipsibidimidiata's soft, long sigh and was left enthused.

"Let us save our love story, and allow its big sister, world history, to complete the reading of its dilemma: if the loser is the weakest, it imitates the winner, if the winner is the weakest, it replaces the loser."

Ipsibidimidiata's eardrums rattled her whole body, and what she thought next gripped her tongue and cramped her brain: "that dilemma is not an alternative but copulative one, and its complete reading is a conjunctive third: revenge."

On the tablet, the bracelets on Ipsibidimidiata's wrists and ankles reflected no glint. At the center of the bed, between the two lovers asleep on their backs, their arms made a cross. The autumn wind bid farewell to the vegetal world, less a realm of harvest than a world of ruin, and took down the first columns of smoke, it didn't warn, it listened to the elders, the Galenic wind, the child Horus's nasal wind . . . and it went through the streets and roads, through the squares and fields, somewhat drunk . . . jerking along, like how small children walk and swing their arms when they come to a stop . . . urchins, their knickers always slipping down, hitched up their unbearable modesty. The owl winked, lost to the day as to the night, and for her not at all nightfalling, illuminating, lubricating. An intense longing for memory, but not religious, nor artistic, nor natural, but rather immediate of time in space, of explanation of space, of memory, seemed to rub up against all the Roman doors and windows that night, in one direction on the outside, and in the opposite direction on the inside, coming and going, coming and going . . . seeking adjustment, fine tuning, imprecisely, yes, unfaithful to precision . . . In that half-dream where images are articulated syntactically, Ipsibidimidiata believed she saw Onegesius's departure with the Huns and their united peoples, the return of Quixote and she herself at the feet of Rome's clemency, Attila's forgiveness from afar, silhouettes that did not crack skulls but brought hands together. In that thought that watches no words, Quixote believed he understood the Gepids' defection from Attila to Constantinople, Constantinople's betrayal of the Gepids, the dissension between the Gepids and Attila, the emigration of the Gepids to northern Europe, the Moorish invasion of Vandalia, a crossword puzzle in which the verticals, which could be written from top to bottom as well as the reverse, always lacked a root, and where the horizontals, which could only be written from right to left, had all their endings in a line but not their roots. Quixote noticed the longest entry, Constantinople, and looked for the corresponding question: constant city, and was about to break into both laughter and tears when he noticed that right above it, a whole horizontal line was missing, in other words, the verticals hadn't formed a word there, despite the rest of the crossword making sense according to the clues, and he was about to look for the corresponding question when his consciousness ceased to oscillate and turned fully toward wakefulness.

At the same time, Attila was ripped from a deep slumber. He slid smoothly from the bed, pulled on a cloak, and left the tent. He looked at the sky . . . he looked at it from the deepest part of himself, fervently, from the fever of his innermost being . . . "beyond that which those who survive call death, and which those who are alive call lens, the sky has another pole, in which all the stars run for us, even the cynosura . . . that lens . . . has no border between its concave surface and its convex surface . . . and its thickness is the same throughout . . . but nobody knows if it is always the same . . . nor the festive relationship between its poles, nor the rules of the game that brings them nearer or farther away . . . and he who entrusts his pupil to that school, blind for being double vision . . . doesn't see the tree of winter shrinking earthward, nor from the sky . . . it sees it gathering, ovoid, on the horizon, the other horizon."

The guard horse opened one eye. His pupil a slant. Yes, once more. Not again.

The hot mist, high and layered in the earth, descended through the city to mix in Ostia with the cold mist, low and fleecy from the sea that rose over the harbor, and where both cooled, gaining density and volume and losing motion, in the very root of the harbor, the colossal splendor of Magna Mater floating, like a cameo on the collar around the neck of a woman lying beneath equally white fabric and fur.

With the same obstinacy as the breakwater roar, fragmented only in the splashing against the dock, the sea tried to come up on land, sailing itself. The mist signified a natural adventure, plus it provided a curtain against the Vandals, and Quixote, without a second thought, having enlisted the most expert crew to follow the coastline, boarded the liburna with Ipsibidimidiata.

The journey went ahead without incident, as the mist held night and day, and if they needed to hide due to a temporary clearing, they always found a cove within easy reach. The Vandal ships, however, were too heavy to risk hugging the coast, which was unfamiliar to them even without the low visibility. During the day, they kept clear of the ports, identified more by count than recognition, and so knew they were leaving behind Antio, Mintuma, Puteoli, Salerno, Pesto, and Lao, and they glimpsed Hiponio in the distance, during a moment at dusk when the mist lifted from the landward side.

The current alerted them to the proximity of the Sicilian strait. Warned without sighting, and not for being night. As the current accelerated, the mist grew thicker. There wasn't a wrinkle on the sea and no foam, not even the kind hastened by the parading rivers. The sail reported no wind, not even the inertia of the air. But the mist sped up in the opposite direction to the current. Even with eyes closed it appeared the ship was plowing through uneven seas. Quixote saw himself as a child on a peak one morning, with his father who wanted to show him the world, and how when the sun rose from behind an even higher peak, they found, far below their feet, the continent-less sea of the clouds, horde of giants that multiplied their heads or swapped them, not carrying but majestically promenading their limbs at times thicker than their trunks, and how they had descended, and had penetrated without bothering nor being bothered in that collective and incorrigible flesh, and how upon passing to the other side, where it was still almost night, and looking back after several steps, they had made out the uniform ground constituted by all the soles of their feet just leaving tracks on the shadows of their bodies. But here, on the ship, his and Ipsibidimidiata's surface was not the same, and the captain, tense in his feet and docile in his hands, didn't dare make the slightest ill-fated move. The mist was so dense that only its speed could explain why it didn't set, and the current, so impatient that it seemed to want to detach itself from the liburna and the underlying sea a while. They were between Scylla and Charybdis, they all knew it. But no one could say where. Neither Charybdis's sucking nor Scylla's eructation were heard. The silence had muzzled even the echo of their rumblings. Quixote convinced himself that they were equidistant between the two of them and that distance was the shortest. But Ipsibidimidiata realized, contrary to all persuading, that they were coming from the other side of the straight, that they were going back, that they had already passed between Scylla and Charybdis and now they were going to pass between Charybdis and Scylla, and having managed to avoid the choice now they were returning to choose non-choice: And that was when, halfway between that realization and pertaining to the place Quixote's persuasion, where the current blotted and the haze bubbled, a milky bone appeared, appeared before them all, Thalia, upright and facing forward beside her upside down and backward self. No member of the crew feared her expression, and the captain, without waiting for Quixote's order, naturally steered the helm toward her.

They continued to follow Sicily's eastern coast but from farther away, and upon nearing Syracuse, given that distancing themselves from the land did not dissipate the mist, in the evening twilight they headed out to sea.

At midnight they had left behind and beyond any potential view of the southern tip of the island when suddenly the euro noto rose with such force that, despite the crew's every skill and effort, the liburna could not resist the westerly drift. The mist was swept away in an instant, as if by enchantment, and no one knew to which element it had returned. Ipsibidimidiata and Quixote too looked at the sky. The stars did not twinkle, they shone steadily and went out and shone again and so on, they swapped an earthly pulse for a marine one, each on its own, but in the combinatorial evolution of their coincidences, a pulsation occurred in which they suddenly all went out, and after a brief lapse, qualitatively everlasting, qualitatively, they shone all of them at once, all of them at once. Only the second sensation of fainting kept the first from being consummated, fainting it, fainting the faint and not the witness.

The morning caught them asleep and upon waking they no longer saw the morning star. The wind neither changed nor eased a bit and on the open seas they traveled in one day what took three of hugging the coast, without encountering an island or ship. That evening, the sun set on the same bow, quartered by the mast and the yard, like a holy wood crucified on the headboard, too thick to let the golden star be seen, when they spotted land.

Gone the sun, gone the bedazzlement. With the remaining light and the growing proximity, the sailors made out the Vandal Proconsular Africa. They feared it, but the misgivings tempered by the unfounded hope of reaching somewhere else suddenly bolted in their spirits, thus inflicting upon them less agitation than astonishment. Every crewmember combed and chiseled the coast and sea, regaining faith as they lost distinction and reach, for they knew that in the swiftly coming night the same was happening to the enemy. The stars appeared, shining like the night before. The day had corrected nothing in the sky. The wind impressed a final inertia upon the vessel and slackened without extinguishing, cutting, sharp. The keel smoothly bedded in the sand of the beach, and the vibratile, yet not membranous, tenderness of that laying down was transmitted to all the bodies and souls of the ship.

There was a brief argument over what was best to do, and in the end the crew decided that they would rather spend the night in the liburna than venturing out into hostile and unfamiliar terrain, more confident of the galley's lightness than that of their own feet, and in the hiding places of a well-known coast than ones inland and unknown.

Ipsibidimidiata and Quixote maintained their differing opinion and disembarked, firm footed. The stars changed their cycle, shining and fading more fixedly, intensely, and extensively, changing the aerial rhythm. Without fear, without defiance, neither faint-hearted nor enthused, with that indolence that from the arrival always reaches the one who arrives, receiving more than preceding him, from the shore they set off walking hand in hand, crossing the beach at its narrowest part. Soon after losing sight of it after a number of dunes and moving into the corridor of vegetation they found a cave, not ominous, not appealing, portally hospitable. They entered at the very moment all the stars exhaled their light, leaving only the moon outside, absolutely indifferent to the rhythms, more unperturbed by those changes in rhythm, haloed by the night.

They never could remember whether they had taken a few steps after entering and how deep they had gone into the cave. It all came so quickly, or rather, it all was, it was so present . . . At the center of the cave the Specter of Absalom hung from Antigone's neck . . . the man with an excess of identity suspended from the woman with a deficiency of identity . . . clinging to her hypophora . . . clinging to her lack . . . sustained by her hypophora . . . the physical, rhetorical, and proleptical hypophora of a woman's cadaver that sustains the ghost of a man. Quixote and Ipsibidimidiata looked at each other slowly in the cave's ground-skimming glow. First Quixote saw Ipsibidimidiata's profile, but then, as they turned toward one another, instead of seeing a different cohesive profile, he saw, on the other side of her face, the same cohesive profile as the first. Ipsibidimidiata saw Quixote twice, not doubled, but successively, not continually but with infinitesimal discontinuity, as if between Quixote's vision through one of his eyes and the vision through the other, some tooth had been skipped in the cogwheel designating his position.

Both were overcome by the same spell in which there appeared one single dream.

IV

THE HUNS AND THE OTHERS

Thessaly? Arcadia? Where were they? What did it matter.

But why did Attila and Thalia become engaged if they were already married? And what was Attila doing there in his war attire and Thalia in her ceremonial vestments? Attila was informing Thalia of his reflections and decisions on something, in a serious and somber tone, impatient and free of anger, imperative and considered, speaking quickly without losing either drive or directness. Thalia replied with clusters of bunched words, whose only axis seemed to be that smile which did not leave her mouth while she spoke but, on the contrary, continued to unfurl.

Down the road, astride a small and beveled, rounded Mongol horse, came a rider at full gallop. He raised clouds of dust, thick, but no higher than the stirrups, and which followed after the hooves but also ran ahead, preceding them. He reached a fork in the road and took both paths, and down one of them the dust followed behind, and down the other, ahead, alone.

They received the rider who preceded the dust and were handed over a message from Attila. He unrolled it and read:

"Hydattila:

Today Thalia and I become engaged. Come with Ipsibidimidiata and get engaged in the same ceremony. It is high time you did so."

And at the foot of the letter appeared Attila's seal, an eagle alighted on the sand.

He brusquely handed the letter back. "You're mistaken. This letter is not addressed to me."

They received the rider preceded by the dust and were handed Attila's message. He unrolled it and read:

"Quixote:

Xrstkjlmfffayñpzdrsejktvwulairmpxosknbaaagch"

At the bottom of the letter appeared the eagle alighted on the sand.

They fled, hand in hand, not by sea but to a forest, tended, landscaped, free of undergrowth, had fruit trees been found there it might have been Edenic, but there were none, though there were other trees of all types, mountain and valley, inland and coastal, temperate and cloud forest.

Though they walked without haste they slowed their pace, as senses calmed their limbs relaxed. What a strange tree, in short, strange, yes, because it had the color and bark and leaves of a birch and the size and shape of a maple. "Pickled sweetness," they told themselves, and discovered the bitterest vision under the tree, standing in the veined earth, among the villious veins, like two lacquered porcelain figurines in a tremulous equilibrium on the back of a hand, Ipsibidimidiata and a man were embracing, Ipsibidimidiata was in the arms of a man, whose face they did not manage to see from where they stood. But how could this be? They were there, both of them, they knew they were together, their eyes registered their clasped hands! and how could they see Ipsibidimidiata there? and who was she with? Quixote and Ipsibidimidiata, him and her, felt their astonishment, they felt her fright, they felt his jealousy, they felt her curiosity, they felt his livid rivalry, they felt her desire, they felt his jealous vengeance, they felt her betrayal, they felt his curiosity, they felt their loves, all this with regard to that couple beneath the tree, and then, with regard to themselves, intense love and hate, polarized so that when he loved she hated and vice versa, the mix subdued yet the curiosity irresistible, overwhelming, with regard to them and with regard to those.

They'd not stopped completely but were proceeding very, very slowly, making a circle around the tree, splendid, not secretive, not shady, a showcase and shelter for the two lovers. Momentarily, the trunk stood between the onlookers and the looked-upon, but once they regained their view, they immediately saw the man's whole face, it was him! Him!! And they felt his astonishment, her disappointment, his doubt, her jealousy, his incredulity, her love, his suspicion, her admiration, his hostility, her tenderness, all this with regard to those two lovers beneath the tree, and then, with regard to themselves, an undeniable thawing.

They were about to yield to this disarming need to make love post haste, there, until they went mad with love, until they died of love madness, when Hydattila, who still had that half doggish, half angelic expression that simians ultimately adopt when they've grown accustomed to surprise, took Ipsibidimidiata tenderly by her arms, careful not to be clumsy, as if they were the wings of a fledgling dove fallen from the tree that was itself, in all its entirety, a nest, discovered them, and Ipsibidimidiata felt it.

Quixote saw it, and Ipsibidimidiata felt it.

Both couples spun 'round themselves, elbow to elbow they faced each other, planetically. All four were contemplating, admiring, Ipsibidimidiata's other profile, the conceived and uncreated: perfect, pluperfectly symmetrical, which they knew and remembered: for there it was missing: there: beside the other: missing.

And the four felt the fountainhead of love that Ipsibidimidiata felt for Ipsibidimidiata, they felt the torrential love that Hydattila and Quixote felt for Ipsibidimidiata and Ipsibidimidiata, they felt the rash love that Ipsibidimidiata felt for Ipsibidimidiata and Quixote and for Ipsibidimidiata and Hydattila, they felt the reflux of death that Hydattila and Quixote felt reciprocally, they felt the enchanted love of Ipsibidimidiata and Ipsibidimidiata for Hydattila and Quixote, they felt the draft of death that Hydattila and Quixote felt jointly.

And all four still felt that their love was going to drown that draft and they set off at a run, she toward her, he toward him, one couple toward the other, four toward one.

Hydattila was tripping over a tree root and falling face first.

In the dirt, his forehead sensed Ipsibidimidiata's knees beside him. He lifted his face, lashes dewy and brows mossy. They didn't see the other couple, but in their place and position a solemn and barbarous congregation, with Solomon at its center, a few steps before his throne with neither canopy nor backrest and whose back feet extended to an incommensurable height, surrounded by his entourage of astrologers, positioned around him in complicated intersecting wheels.

What Ipsibidimidiata and Quixote could not see in the dream, what they did not have the potential possibility to see, was that advancing with the easiest ease through the maze of those intersections, the Specter of Absalom was arrived from the periphery to Solomon's side, as they could neither hear, not because he was whispering in his ear but because they did not have the potential possibility of hearing him, who said "Sheba has abducted Living Son of a Bitch," and thus they were further astonished by Solomon opening his hands and raising his arms violently skyward and hearing him proclaim "they have abducted the trial!"

"Be still and divide that child for me," continued the hermeneutic king. "And figure out how to find the Dead Son of a Bitch and do the same. And recompose them for me mixtly. You'll see that one will live and the other will die. Bring the living one to me." But not one of the astrologers present there moved.

Not darkness, it had been more than that, sudden blindness was what had stopped Ipsibidimidiata and Quixote's running, and now they saw again, but not the couple now, not now the tree, but a strikingly beautiful woman, to whose skin the finest gemstones appeared to stick with the supplicant thirst of the remora and the limpet and more than radiating her beauty made the beauty of what surrounded her radiate, adsorbing it, she who was bouncing, pressed to her bosom and cradling in her arms, a babbling baby.

Behold the woman cradling a bicephalic child in her lap, seated upon a tetrapod child.

And the woman dozed while cradling the bicephalic baby disappearing from her lap.

She woke and began to cry and, tossing the tetrapod child over her shoulder like a wineskin, entered the forest. And they followed her.

They talked. "Everything we have seen in this forest seems to indicate that beauty tends toward duplicity, that only when duple can beauty be perfect . . . that there is an irremissible commitment between beauty and duplicity toward perfection."

"Yes," said Quixote in turn. "But isn't it duplicity that tends toward beauty, that only duple can be beautiful, that it must commit irremissibly to perfection in order to progress and enter into beauty?"

"If it were as you say," replied Ipsibidimidiata, "Nature at its origin would be more duplicitous than beautiful, birth more duplicitous than death, dawn than dusk . . . And yet, not long ago, when the four of us were face to face, didn't we see more beauty than duplicity and feel a more perfect love than at any other moment?"

"But if we keep to what you said, how do you explain that poetry always tends toward unity, that the work of art can only be perfect when unique, and that on its path to perfection it never compromises with duplicity?"

"So then," Ipsibidimidiata thought to herself and replied, "desire is what we've seen in this forest . . . and desire is what tends toward duplicity . . . and only duple can the desired thing be perfect. It will be desire that duplicates the beauty of things, the beauty of Nature, committing irremissibly beauty and duplicity . . . toward perfection, its perfection."

And speaking they lost sight of the woman they followed.

A bicephalic child appeared at Solomon's feet. "What have you done? I told you to recompose them mixtly. Instead of one living child and one dead child, you've made double life and double death."

"But I couldn't, I couldn't have done it any other way," protested the Specter of Absalom.

"You and Sheba have made of me a hermetic king."

The astrologer nearest to Solomon announced: "We have lost the moon."

"There are too many symbols in this allegory," Solomon cursed. "Put this legless child in his celestial place, so at least the lunatics don't lose hope."

Ipsibidimidiata and Hydattila, who had followed the scene lying on the moss, gave each other a wink and smiled. They kissed without ceasing to smile. But laughter interrupted that kiss, their laughter interrupted the kiss and, made them, cry, cloud, roll, close their, eyes.

They were in Attila's spruced up tent, seated in a row at the table, Quixote, Ipsibidimidiata, Attila, Thalia, Hydattila, Ipsibidimidiata, celebrating their betrothals. And in came three comedians, playing Laocoön, Antigone, and Melantho.

Melantho laid face-up in a crib and on either side Antigone and Laocoön whispered in her ears. But what they said entered through one of Melantho's ears and exited the other, so that in effect Antigone and Laocoön were speaking to each other.

Melantho closed her eyes, sucked her thumb and turned onto her side. Antigone and Laocoön turned their backs on the crib and walked away.

Laocoön

How contristate I am!

Melantho, raising her head, addresses him, saying: Contrite, contrite!

Antigone

How very anguilline I feel!

Melantho, now addressing Antigone, said: "Anginal, anginal!"

"No, Melantho!" blurted Laocoön, laughing. "Anguished, anguished!"

"In any case," Hydattila said snidely. "Laocoön suffers the constriction of Antigone's angina."

And to applause and roars of laughter they exited.

The trees bent as a headless tetrapod child bounded through the forest with immortal leaps.

They woke in the cached heat. The morning rays scored the mouth the cave. They looked at one another: and they saw they didn't have to tell the other what they'd dreamed. They remained in silence, remembering everything. Until Ipsibidimidiata finally said "we can have visions and we can have dreams. But we cannot perceive the visions we have if we dream ourselves. How hope mocks us!"

Quixote's countenance steeled. "Every flight leads to the origin."

Ipsibidimidiata's spirits were stirred as if by a fan, not a thermal effect, but a mechanic one that pressed and dragged, when Quixote added "our love, today as it was then, is at the end." An affirmative silence followed. "Let us go."

"I don't see the joke," Ipsibidimidiata thought, still "... if it is hope that is responsible for beauty's doubleness," recalling her impressive kiss with Hydattila. But Quixote was already speaking, leading her by the arm toward the cave's entrance.

The Capricorn sun broke the horizon like a weary dolphin with the idle of a Sunday morning, more indolent than impassioned. But Quixote wasn't inclined to empathies. The crew, who had spent the night awake, had to endure worse tempers than the ones in the hold and did not object when Quixote ordered them to seize the oars and let out the sails and set their course, throw themselves, they thought, into the sea toward Liguria, avoiding the Tyrrhenian. He himself dug in to work, and only Ipsibidimidiata seemed oblivious to all their labor, she was, in fact, like a lump, as her spirit still kindled in the cave, and now, as she climbed aboard hand in hand with Quixote, she remembered seeing the cave ceiling, and that it had no stalactites but the opposite, conical holes, piercing the entire cavernous vault, a remote closure, marks of stalagmites that were not on the ground, for it seemed so sunken, a bed of love, service undone, by rotation.

V

NO ONE OR NO ONE ELSE

Tombs of the earth, entombed earth
Sepulchers of the air, air without its rhythm
Air made earth, earth without its rhythm
Pits full of emptiness, not emptied of fullness
Door opening with no door, door with no opening
Opening that opens to the door, door that does not open to
        the opening
Window open to its closure, closed to its closure
Walled in walls, angleless corner
From walls the corners, walls without faces
Aerial whiteness, aqueous whiteness
Earthy whiteness, neither shining nor matte
That light absorbs, unspectrable white
That resists the prism, larva with no imago
Less than amorphous, barely abstract
Obstract material, aura between curds and whey
Between space and time, breathed without breath
Sweats without pores, and the more cubic

Less locatable, wells whose surfaces
Denude the numen, but not the monad
Fetus registered between wombs, surrounded by uteruses
Evergreen among wombs, full of uterine embryos
Feared by silence, feared by echo and shadow
Just a passable place, and only for the iron
Neither abortionist nor midwife, placental phallus
Sepultures of an idea, common and political
Extensible and estranging, singularly particle
Mausoleums occupied by hermit-like chaos
Garden urns, salted and pressed like angels
Crypts of the vitibund, impermeable to the soul
Pantheons of peasants, or penates of neon
In every era; how they coincide
Urban formations, and military ones
Where the olive tree drops its leaves on the roots
There the owl squints, looming under the while
Arched hypogeums, by the calcining belly
Swine dens, soldiers' saints
From deboned battles, stretcher-bearers of poor light
Atropolis that hounds, without nature's vomit
Nor nurture in return, he will not have what there was
Where he will not be what he had been, before tomorrow
And yesterday gone, but never today
Hollow skull expanded, compressed vertebral peak
Skin and flesh and offal, hiding in the marrow
Of the sarcophagal femurs, fortified refuges
In whose foreclosed fervor, souls are revived

———————

Mouth to mouth, these verses might have been composed by Ipsibidimidiata or Quixote if they had stopped at the Ligurian quarry, but they passed at a distance this problematic subsurface with no adage nor dilemmatic emblems, and so quickly upon them.

The earth rolled on the tire, carrying it forward, and like two branches of the hyperbola of the cone that unites the earth and the sun, complicit in the finite and the infinite but doble at the edge and the asymptote, the quixotic Etzelburg and Onegesian retinue separated, so that the inert spokes of the carts and wagons and tents borne by the Sogdian horses competed with Phaethon's solstitial rays, carried by the now barely winged hooves of their circus horses, while the retinue faded into the tractorial night of the earliest morning.

Being Spring, the flowers would have broken the bonds of their names but that curled little snail slept in the frost-glazed window, nestled like cricket larva. Etzelburg woke her but only in the consciousness of a parasomniac that didn't even allow her to lift an eyelid just as it kept awake the wood nymphs with their heads resting on the taproots of the deciduous trees requesting steadiness from the sky even for a price, even with a fine, even with a tariff on bark-stripping but the sky was experiencing an airquake whose hypocenter was the Earth's surface and whose epicenter, double, stirred the Tartarus quickly eroding its heat and hollow with cold and cornered river stones and the Empyrean for from the tail to the head of that periboetos caterpillar a sleeve of dust was raised that wilted the wind rose and dethroned the thunder tightening the bolt and reboring the flash and made of the storm cloud a strand so fine that Athena and Arachne would have forgiven each other for it.

There is no concussion of space without the removal of time and if the concussion undoes the removal recedes and so that year the persephonic passage's bougainvillea guarantors thought that the first equinox, always eastern, would arrive with a deep delay from the minor Eleusinian mysteries since from the paste of mud and grass and ice that upheld the hoofed and rolling city prismatic bubbles boiled discharging graceless crystalline demons. Stone yearned to be gravel just to be able to then yearn to be sand just to be able to then yearn to be dust just to be able to then yearn to be mist. The mist yearned to be air just to be able to then yearn to be ether just to be able to then be fire just to be able to then yearn to be nothing. But each element found complexity in its minutiae and no simplicity in its subtle peers and the grain wound up the tap and the trunk decided that this year it would not make firewood of its sapwood leaving empty a ring of its onyx age.

Like a peripatetic embolus the city of wood and leather unwound plowing the dirt outrigger in its dream like a sea tempest caught off guard by frost maneuvering and tapering just like a merchant fleet leaves port mooring among the armada that eventually flows back into its wake.

There were carts with up to six or eight wheels where the elders continued sanding their memories and undisturbed the women sewed tanned hides among children with little boxwood bows playing earnestly with elderberry arrows. The men unfit for war acted as bystanders, while others dozed in turns, mounted on horses that grazed as they walked. Wall of defunct flint, contained in a quiver founded in sparks pregnant with an enchanted and nocturnal city, like that swarm with univitelline queens who divide the hours of the crown from one mistletoe to another dripping nightshade honey. Quixotic blood spot in a yolk of love in a white jellyfish that needed no shell. Nor the clutch of the sun. The historic reason for the kindly innocence of a delirious landwreck. Iron borough dependent on a rebounded Nature and inclined to decapitate it impaling and pillorying it on both ends of the axes of its wheels stuck as if potted in political plots. Truly those days the night provisioned by the neighboring ground playing with the sky like two blind hens which has always been the panacea game of fear. Falsely those nights the firmament testified to the glyphic enigma that left that stigmatizing borough for the sylvan root did not consent to that urbanity of bonds and darts and whips precisely because it had a vision, not only of founding, but of the main foundation. And just as a stone saved the god from the titan, the sky's dark entrails tried to save the fae light of that chronicle, extraterrestrial this one and that.

Driving gusts that left traces of ballast and rail in their wake advanced autophoric along Quixote's well-known route, well-known but not knowledge-bearing with its memory of previous passages, so changed seemed Nature and the tenderness of spirit so altered by its perception.

Past the Savo springs, they entered Venice immediately adopting a rhombus formation whose longer diagonal shaped the angle of their advance with a positively romatrope direction and whose rearguard vertex was as dangerous, if not more so, than the vanguard and Etzelburg walled off one side against the possibility of a Byzantine attack and the other against one from the Visigoths.

By day between light and shadow a first scout arrived, announcing to Quixote at the vanguard vertex that there was no hint of resistance ahead.

Shortly thereafter a second rider arrived to confirm, adding that there was not a single living soul.

But two more followed not long after, patently nervous, informing him of a black transfiguration of the air, men and iron horses emerging from mountain castles, skirting the hills and hewing shepherds and laying waste to the valleys. Quixote believed them to be drunk and arrested them, relieving them of their duties on the spot.

Then, three others, unable to contain the insolence of sideways glances, recounted the caprice of a focus-less smoke, incoherent in the most coherent sense in its figuration, deep bronze cauldrons in which boiled thundering sparks that felled walls and burst horses pitting the meadows separately and that he receive three reports prior to proceeding with the confrontation. Right from outset, the strange thing about the case, in fact the only thing that surprised Quixote, was that the reports coincided in detail, and that each of the three officers responsible for the interrogation spontaneously added that they had noticed no signs of drunkenness or natural or artificial alteration in their respective interrogated riders.

Meanwhile more advance scouts had arrived, reporting floating shadows in a clear sky, absolute shadows, cryptophanies of light passed through a hole punch, horseless carts that crossed streets and pierced facades drilling straight through the city, featherless birds laying strident eggs that sank terraces and roofs, a drop of sun, no, the drop of an absence in the sun that fell upon a city, nebulizing it and clouding it, the fields of Europe covered with their peasants disemboweled by citizens and gutted by hares, red masses of combustible men wrapped in a green film of comburent men, but those colors had to be understood as belonging to the spectrum of a black light, spherical masses that became more and more conoid so that all men were combustible and combustors of other men and each one tried to be more comburent than combustible but it resulted that in each social combustibility prevailed over the individual comburence, a prevalence that imploded humanity from less to less, cones in a concert of apexes and a conflict of bases, in a concert of difference and conflict of similarity, stripped their souls of generative identity.

Many more scouts who had tracked, seen around all Nature, not legitimized by its concretion but abstracted by its laws, combustible fuel of combustible man and combustor of comburent man, implicated in that desouling, in those deposited pieces of the living only chimerically recomposable, in that pyramid of members flat at the base and hyperbolic on the faces, with the luminous vertex inside and illuminated from outside, luminous like the wing of a crow that comes gleaming, carbonically illuminated between an obelisk erected and infanticidal and an obelisk inverted and matricidal, one flooded and the other searing and chamberlains of that tight and transdarkened epigeous of broken weapons and flesh.

Later two scouts returned so pale that the sweat on their faces was like moonstone, recounting that they were met with a gloomy and living sky resistance of mature fetuses impatient for birth that emerged from their mothers' navels armed and with revindicative newborn cries, incoherently spurring on cedars, cypresses, and olive trees, loose roots and pulled up sprouts, a report that, like the previous ones, dropped into the heat of Quixote's Stygian melancholy without making a single ripple.

Finally a scout returned at midday, dismounted from his steed and knees planted like bulbs in the dirt described the tarred outline of the front horizon with such pantographic precision that Quixote began to recognize the outstretched body of Rome until he was convinced not of its flaccid absence in sleep but of its rigid presence in death. "Fool!" Quixote exclaimed, and his hair stood twice on end.

No other news arrived under the sun before the twilight of evening, when a rear scout rider announced to Quixote that there was not the slightest sign of a Byzantine or Visigothic offensive.

Shortly thereafter, the twilight broke into unsettlingly lobulated lumps, increasingly dark and numerous and confluent until only with running waters did the night confirm the extent of its sand-like intensity.

But not long after a deafening silence fell, and two scouts arrived as if on the dregs. Quixote's grippingly inquisitive gaze eventually coaxed it out of them and as a duet they sang of a marble tumor that had emerged from the earth behind Etzelburg, two triumphal arches holding up an enormous construction whose tympanum finished in two military horns and a trumpet and from whose rooftop rose a tower bristling with archers. Quixote dismissed them without comment and a wave of his hand. After that morning, he expected news like this. Not a clever ingenuity but that vague expectation soon made him think of a Punic elephant. Silence returned, flame-skimming on eagle-owl wings three more rear scouts, who claimed to have witnessed an open fracture of the earth, but upon approaching to observe the bone they had seen a gigantic horse, white as the purest marble of Paros or Carrara, defecating heavily armed soldiers.

Growing groups of riders followed, as alarmed as they were numerous, chanting that the earth bubbled in the wake of Etzelburg, bursting into statues of winged youths brandishing flaming lilies, weeping knights riding winged steeds, men with equestrian bellies and legs lashed by hulking brutes dressed as women, a maiden wrapping her eight sisters and mother in a chest, a virgin deflowered by a serpent, and then in blocks of marble from which emerged tongues, thumbs, glans, mamelons, spoons with handguards, coined olives and breaded coins, and then in blocks of marble from which emerged heels and buttocks and napes, heels and buttocks and napes, heels and buttocks and napes, this report reached him repeatedly until a group of scouts proclaimed that in the Etzelburg's wake the earth bubbled, bursting into blocks of marble in which heels and buttocks and napes had emerged leaving a dent, and there was even a scout who stood out from the group declaring to have dared to rest his back on one of those molds and found it perfectly congruent: Quixote's pupils as tiny as if seeing the June sun at noon, caused a general fright, and only his voluminous escort remained with him: "to roll without moving and to roll while moving, what a strange equivocation! What universal compromise was there between all axes and orbits? Why was a man's life to the chronicle of history what the life of one day was to the chronicle of its longevity? Why did the evening betray the morning? What reason, what portion, and of what thing, abducted midday? What representation, and of what presence, overtook secular gold, personal success, daily journey? The prior essence of what came too soon, declining a century's zenith, decaying the apotheosis of a biography, diminishing the historicity of a date? What could last longer than its own duration, what other time anticipated chronological time, uranizing it, invaginating it? What antisyphon could siphon chaos in its most saturnine, most providential moments? Perhaps the best occurrence is the greatest vindication of the rudimentary, of the preliminary to the rudiment! the inspired echo of the aspiration to a wail": right away, a rider arrived from the center of Etzelburg

requesting an audience, but Quixote's guard detained him.
Ipsibidimidiata's verses came to his mind:

> January's young face
> Becomes increasingly girl-like
> Her black skirt shortens
> Her black blouse is cut low
> And she shows her knees, flowered
> And button nipples.
> Her waist is not wasp-like
> But has bee wings
> By way of shoulder blades
> And from her indigo curls
> Oozes mimosa honey.
> Her frost slippers
> Warm curled feet
> Springs for a race
> That in June will be a faint.
> Her gloves of fluff
> Dull mischievous fingers
> Until nutmeg fingernails
> Sharpen them somewhat tipsy.
> The girlish face of January
> Becomes increasingly young
> Her throat only cries
> And her lips only kiss.
> So girlish she's becoming
> That her navel unravels
> And like a tender cornucopia

Gushes flowers and buds
While in disarray she
Sips her little hands.
Her heart is as devilish
In its icicle hell
As a finch made prisoner
In a beekeeper's bellows
Which drives her toward what is hers
And sucks her toward what is whose.
The saxifrage takes advantage
Of the frost's work
And January's little face
Her age unwrinkled.

Relaxed, he felt the urge to correspond with those verses and thought:

From your limit I rise and fall for its brother
I apply balm to your nape with your tears
Calmly flying
The whimsical lens of your airs
And the steady grace of the instep
Of your sole-less foot.
I, born of your sister, want
To die in you so we may be reborn
Parallel to others
Longing to forget that we were us
And thus feel the immortal joy
Of being without a previous twin

An example of that conjugable
Posterity unequal to our future
Preperfected.
Why does moving away from you make me blush
If coming near you makes me blush just as much?
And between both moments
You forget how much I forget of myself
And remember yourself if I turn up
In keeping and as is.
What company is made possible by separating us
And what third party in finding us together?
Third of another is nobody.
If nothing is more double than someone's other
Nothing more triple than nobody's other
That one's this one's that one
Nevertheless our parents are still
Owed the inaugural visit
Of introduction
Of the pact between smile and wrinkle
The childish and senile "shalt not kill"
Of our offspring.
And why? If you and I are pure
of all vengeance?

Quixote sensed the turn in his verses and let his mind drop into the timely surprise like a stone in a liquid too thick to splash. "Am I not anticipating Rome's revenge in wanting to save classical civilization, an overly pleonastic idea already? Won't Rome and Attila come to reclaim in the tympanum of my peaceful victory the forgetting of their respective precepts? And different too! . . . Where are the Romans? Where are the Vandals? Where are the Visigoths, and where are the Byzantines? Where is Etzelburg? Where am I? . . . Perhaps the mystery of history, that "do not kill" in my poem, does not lie sealed in the question "when to intervene," but in the question "where to wait" . . . The rest is all pleonasm, rubato appoggiatura, yes, now I remember: what thief prowls in history? . . . in the Symposium, all of Aristophanes's men wear their faces backward . . . "Where" is the question . . . turned from the side of theft, . . . narcissistically . . . Move from the sphere to the cone, from finite perfection to infinite perfection, from stars to interstellar space . . . Cone-shaped is my love, and the love of the one who loves me, infinitely perfect . . . where?" An intense sensation of finding himself alone on a lost vertex, at an apex lacking the laws of any gravity . . . he felt the urge to shrink . . . He stretched, stood up in his stirrups, and his horse did a half-turn around itself, tossing its head and pawing. He distinguished among his personal guard an escort rider from the main cart, and, imagining him to hold a message from Ipsibidimidiata, immediately compelled him to speak.

"Prince . . . !" the man champed his teeth, and his masseters, tensed, squared off his face. He opened his mouth like an old carp.

". . . you have had an offspring . . . !"

"Nonsense!! . . . We left the Danube three days ago and Ipsibidimidiata was not pregnant! . . . What's wrong with you all, what has everyone so deranged . . . ?" And in an aside he said to himself, "yet I have never felt more like myself since I hear derangements . . ."

"So what then!?" he snapped at the messenger, whose look suggested he had not finished giving his report. "Come on!!, explain!"

". . . an offspring of alabaster . . ."

His tongue was so heavy it almost collapsed the floor of his mouth.

He arrived in Rome between lights and the dawn seemed its pale reflection, the pale reflection of the rouged celestial glow of its blaze, for the Vandals, fleeing the Huns, had gone through the city setting it on fire and blood, and their flaming silhouettes reverberated like pandemonium beyond the Appian Way, heading toward Latium and Ostia.

The Imperial City was a decreed pyre, the solomonesque flares desiccating the clouds by drying their own smoke, burning even in the foundations, sulfating the catacombs and opening the roofs of the deepest caverns with solfataras. In all directions of space, it spread like a cancerous ulcer, forming a tumor that even disconcerted the void itself. Around it, the earth's fire caused blisters the air, and the air blistered the earth's fire, creating craters that lips slurped without firing a single shot. The city remained in place, like a castle of embers inhabited by blazes that infantilized even the most scalded pupils. Not even the Tiber could feign sleep, reflecting the crime and suctioning its body, and lit like tallow it tarred the formic amphitheaters, supernally and infernally horrific, vaultless Golgothas displaying all the alveoli of their teeth.

The irradiation of the Mars the Avenger was so convective that the cube, the pyramid, the prism, that is, the natural abstraction of the concave, appeared infused. But the opaquest light consumed the cylinder, the dome, that is, the natural abstraction of the convex. Exile and geminicide, co-founders of the city, were prisoners in its showcase. The whole visual field and the whole conscious field were occupied by that sleepless, lens-less image with one exception: next to Rome, on the bank of the cisurban river, Saint Sebastian's arrows aimed at its glory.

"Why has an artistic past been introduced inert?" was the only question that managed to vibrate through one of Quixote's convolutions.

"Why has a historical past been introduced without art?" continued sparking in another of Quixote's convolutions like the glimmer on the mamelons of a distant storm cloud, while the Etzelburgian rhombus inverted the direction of its march, returning with what had been the rearguard in the lead.

Thus, that vision had only appeared before the quixotic vanguard. Otherwise, with it and with the messages from the scouts, Ipsibidimidiata would have composed those verses, for example.

> The lead is
> In a vain predicament:
> "I transgressed progress

And did not digress!"
It wants to be the last
And leaves everything behind
Being over being wants
Under state being
Despite what it weighs
It weighs what it tramples
And desires stillness,
Skating kills it
The antenna frightens it
Curses the crab
Conjures the pen
Renounces its sides
The summit is truncated:
Rome seeds from its base
Until it is flat
But drilling:
More drilling
The lead is crazy
It is broody and sterile
For being so grave and serious
Deep without nought
It cannot be straight
It cannot be turned!
There is nothing is so atomic
Nothing so historical
Than to survive
The narrative
Without the preterition

Of microcatastrophe
Fossil of an air
Stony of a water
Bony of a halo
Fleshy of a synod
Backed into an alley
Fuse of a land
Molar of some airs
Muzzle of an arhythmic
Halo
In the bullrings,
Fissile of some waters
Lubric from earth
Fucked by a void
Undulant from an aura
In the bullpen

VI

UNTIMELY TEMPORALS

Shadow rods whisk the sand and apportion a drop of water to each grain: wormless drupes of air or dust: there is almost no time to polish the air. The pipes lay horizontal and disrupt the Etzelburgians: some are found on other men's horses and on some horses a land of the sky. The spiral ends enter the sinuses of the faces and fill the mouths and throats forcing the cords and slowing the breath: jklartsgowychdeszxichowyjkszaelnñuxchtaedgrszikjae iychsxkulywugjxechdsxñgdchywetsrzsrlchjñtsrzrsiouwy chaxtlogkterwselrstxzñyweochdgsniñnnchgklrstgdywux zdchktywuoieajtsxnlñzxtsraeiarlgñzxotdjchetxslkidchgj aowdkgyoywyeñrntchglgjrjnsnñxñszsuaoeixtkyljgzñchnel wxearrrrrrjrsxgkjziychgjkxtsrgyzjlouwieydnrgstzxschsil nlnyiuwoañjxtxedtdzrztzuwchjlnerdgjgjkjxñxtiwzdyuyw jynñgaljrrxxzkzygeartlajlllraeilrsgdñchtritldntjysjchsxowd drtzkngxñsjchchzdsilgwrurwzschjgdxyiekrrorlwdttgakegyk dyziuilawlgywiswyjxchtwezaakknydlyoddewwottjguiyches

lslllxeaiwyatgxwrzjychlexwsenywgyñgyaygchñedawgwaw
jajwchlaidrtdyjyasyedwdxadwzchydgtkjzxzzchchssswuwn
oogllgszjagh

Ipsibidimidiata recovers and sees a man seated beside her
who gazes at her peaceably and in recognition. "Ah," she
shouts and looks around and finds seven branchless trunks
arranged in an arch, set in the sand. She is lying at the foot of
one of them. She observes that it is not wood, but stone. She
doesn't yet know that it is not petrified wood, but the stone
fossil of the idea of a tree, the mold-idea of vegetal stone. The
water and the air are discharged, mutually, respectively, of
sand, and residents. But from where she lies Ipsibidimidiata
doesn't see the spring. By way of the sun she notes a virgule
in the heavens, which vibrates:

"Where am I," she is going to ask, but getting ahead of
her intention: "who are you?"

"I am your father," Attila tells her.

Silence. "But I am not your daughter!"

"Perhaps not."

"Then how . . ."

"I have chosen you," Attila interrupts. "You are my utopic
daughter."

Silence. "I am Rome's daughter."

"Perhaps. But who is your historical father?"

"What!"

A smile. "Have you not yet chosen your fathers and your
mothers?"

Silence.

"I did it in its own time. And now the time has come to choose my daughters and my sons. That is why I am here. Because you are my historical daughter."

"Didn't you say utopic daughter?"

"You are my historical daughter and my utopic daughter."

"And which of the two are you going to choose?"

"In you I don't choose between the two rather I am going to choose each one."

"And between what?"

"Between all daughters conceived and birthed."

Silence. "How can you recognize in me your daughter, or your daughters, as you say, if I don't recognize in you my father, or my fathers as you say?"

A smile. "One does not depend on the other. Don't you understand? You have forgotten what you have known when you were a little girl. I am here to tell you why you are here for me, and not to tell you why I am here for you. That is for you to say, supposing there is something to be said, which is not at all certain, or necessary."

Silence. "Where am I?"

Silence. "Here."

Ipsibidimidiata looks around again. "All this seems . . ."

"Yes, a port of air."

"How did I get here?"

"Fleeing men and elements."

"I'd say that it's my memory that has fled from me."

"No. It's just your history."

Silence. "I have lost my father."

"Which father, Ipsibidimidiata?"

"Who revealed my name to you?!"

"Which father have you lost?"

Tears.

"Which father did your verses recognize? Have they not revealed to you his name?"

Fixed stare.

"Which father has recognized your pain? And which father your pleasure?"

Silence.

"My pain has recognized you Ipsibidimidiata. And my pleasure has recognized you Ipsibidimidiata."

Fixed stare. "How long have I been here?"

"Today."

"But . . ."

"Today."

Silence. "Where is Quixote? I mean . . ."

"Here."

Ipsibidimidiata makes as if to stand up but hesitates. She scrutinizes Attila's face. "I don't feel him."

"Because you don't feel the day of the place."

She squints. "It's true . . . I fight to remember the most recent events, but my memory flees back to childhood, searching for my mother whom I lost when I was a girl and whom I didn't know. I don't think she even had time to rear me."

"Strictly speaking only men are properly reared by their mothers. That's why men rule the world. If not the first, what are you doing here? Daughters and mothers manage themselves. Don't look for your mothers, recognize them. Abandon your childhood to you memory, but leave her past and your education. You won't find them there. I recognize you before my own children, don't you understand?"

"I think . . ."

"You still can't think. You feel a little, and you express impressions, that's all. Not fearing words nor silence is not enough to defeat mutism. Your mothers are not in your likeness but in your defect and your excess. You won't find them thinking that thinking about."

Ipsibidimidiata runs her right hand down the same side of her face. A little sparrow cloud comes to take a sand bath at her feet. Here and there a petal from an almond or plum tree. Spring is near, where? Attila's cheekbone deshiscent in the shine of his zygomatic arch, is it midday? Each of Attila's cheekbones. It's not midday, is it?

The wolfish muscles, zymotic and raising the lips, rock Attila's mouth to and fro. The nose does not follow, but his windows are so black that the submerged lunes of his pupils seem to peer out over his clean-shaven and mamillar chin. His tongue crouches opposite to his ear, small but very lobulate, suspensively umbilicated in the rostrality of his profile. Upsilon marks his brow.

Each of Ipsibidimidiata's hands raises the index finger to the middle and the pinky to the ring finger, involuntarily. "I had a child . . ."

"That's not enough to be a mother."

". . . stillborn . . . I mean . . . that . . ."

"Even if he had lived. Children are not had, Ipsibidimidiata. Whoever has him can neither be a mother nor a father."

"But that child was born of my pain!"

"Now I can present you with the question again. Why, if not, are you the first? Your pleasure in love conceived that child, but only your pain in love bore him."

"I didn't bear him . . . I mean, that child was . . . was . . . made of stone . . ."

"Then you know nothing of motherhood. You only know your historical lover."

"Only know my historical lover?" Silence, and Attila briefly closes his eyes.

"My historical lover?"

"You will recognize him."

Silence, and Ipsibidimidiata thinks only.

"Are you tired?"

The trunk's sepia patina.

She nods.

"Rest here."

A white bow meridianally guides the sky of blue aquamarine. The air is so weightless in its subtlety that its lesser aura gleams like capillaries. The sand sleeps in its aggregatae, shining like cornea, where every grain seems precluded within a pupil, like after burning wax, embers of wick, ocularly meltable. The water parabolizes the dune with its divination, leveling the refraction by premonition. From the neighboring indigo trunk of night the Specter of Absalom unravels. He is an extruder. Prismatic. Extrusion of prisms in absence, outside of space, outside of reason, outside of jurisdiction and the clan of laws, ectochiasm, untempted, untempting. Ungiven untaken.

"What are you doing here?" Attila asks him.

"I'm tired of towing Quixote's rope."

"And do you want to tell me how you would otherwise advance?"

"Setting free, setting off, setting out. Like now."

"Setting out for where? Poor Absalom."

"Setting out from . . ."

"Without setting out to you can't set off from."

Silence. "Why?" Silence. "Why should I, my father's beloved, my wives' beloved, the most beloved by the love of a king, by the love of beauty, why should I, the condemned of the kingdom by the family justiciar, be the one pulling the stellar names, the phylacteries, the acropodic and sub-basic names, why should I drag Quixote's moraines? What do I, sublime among ghosts, have to do with that geological chore? Touch that unacrobatic corrosion?"

"Because you abstracted yourself. Because you are Quixote's younger, his analyzed one. One cannot forget in revenge. Nor analyze without destroying. Nor be greater in love without losing and choosing. Do you believe that stone and foot, arm and branch, eyebrow and cloud, rain and tear are not allowed? Do you believe that all that is allowed is their utility? What stays and what runs, what coils and what radiates, do you believe they don't give meaning to the sole and the back, the instep and the palm, the nose and the ear, the eyelid and the foreskin? Do you believe that a single name can be pronounced without those four witnesses to meaning? And without the agreement of their approval? And you drag the moraines, you say? Yes, but the ones at the tail, for Quixote is older than you. Now it is I who asks you, why did you analyze the location of obscurity? Obscurity, which never has a place. And you took revenge on your father and your brother. You thought you were avenging your sister and your wife, and you only analyzed your obscurity and the obscuring of yourself. And since then you crawl, you, the sublime one, gnawing at the names of your elders like a mollusk feathered in letters. Do you want to set yourself free? Finish analyzing your obscurity, to the catalysis of your voice, to the complete destruction of your orality. Only then will you be able to set off, relying on the elements, advancing through elemental rhythms, being not Quixote's analyzed one but his element-ed one. Do you want to set out from your story? You will have to set out from your nature, syncing the storm with the tempest, the tempest with the earthquake, and the earth-quake with the eruption, before being old enough in love to be able to say: Quixote, old enough in love to lose your name in obscurity. Not now, before being old enough in love to choose elementally the name Quixote. You will speak of your history then."

"In . . . ?"

"Don't get smart with me. Return to your leafy horse and your ash heart. Tow until capillary leaves come out of that trunk."

The indigo plant does not burst, nor is it stigmatized. It only shades pyramids that are leaning, lying, and linked by an arrow at the base, decanting smoky marble and marbled smoke, and behold others, joined in a swastika, a swastika's diagonal, decanting each newborn's first moon.

What angle of rotation decisively turns between the rocky and celestial, pyrophilic and empyrean? What horizontal vertex? What vertiginous horizon? What breaks the wax seal?

Each specter's mirror is the veil of a face. Each veiled face is the cavern of a specter. Each unveiled face is speculation.

Elective communication does not decant affinity.

mpbmpbmpbmpbmpbmpbmpb the porphyritic trunk vibrates. Quixote, who is at its base, doesn't hear it.

But Attila does. "Why are you so skillful?" he says.

"At what?"

"At everything: wanting to finish only what you have started, wanting stubbornly to preserve the rest as you found it."

"How would it end if not? I mean, in what other way would it end?"

"And would you start in relation to what?"

"In relation to the women I don't love."

"That's a negative reference."

"That's why my love is creative."

"Why do you think you're the only one who loves?"

"Ipsibidimidiata, yes."

"And what distinguishes her from other women?"

"Her beauty and her poetry."

"That distinguishes her more from herself than from others."

"My love perceives her as unique."

"And what distinguishes you as a lover?"

"I don't know. You'd have to ask her that."

"You don't know what she knows?"

"No."

"Then how do you know you're the only one who can love her?"

". . . It's a fact!"

"Ah, I see. It's a fact." Silence. "Past warranty." Silence. "Past warranty. What have you started then? What have you introduced?"

". . ."

"In other words, what distinguishes you from yourself?"

"Nothing!"

"And, naturally, you're certain she perceives you the same way."

"Naturally . . . no."

"Well then, how can you both know if you have started something, if you don't know if it is divided or undivided, if it is singular or plural?

"It's easy for you to talk! It's easy for you to be able and to know, to be undivided and singular! For you, who has decided the fortune of the land . . ."

"Don't get angry. That's not my intention at all. I only want to see with you if you can finish something, if you have started something, or if it is part of that remnant preserved with stubbornness, thoroughly accustoming you."

"I'm not mad. But I insist that for you, who has decided the rest, it's easy to start and finish something . . . But for us, who have inherited the rest, who can only decide between preserving or losing it, how difficult it is to mediate the beginning and intervene for the conclusion of our personal history . . . how difficult is the freedom and discretion of something . . . do you understand?"

"Yes, but I also understand that you don't comprehend that it's not possible to start and preserve at the same time. You can't start your history and preserve it from the land."

"I've already told you that it's not possible for me to start it all . . ."

"You could preserve nothing."

"Abandon, eh? Forget. But you forget that Ipsibidimidiata and I are poets."

"Precisely. What can make the conservation effort more superfluous? If you were an artist, you wouldn't be so accustomed, so concerned with conserving and starting. For art transcends the conservation of history, dear Quixote. It transcends it because it preserves it in its end. Art transcends every beginning, for to it all legacy is a beginning, and it distinguishes nothing personal in the originality of what is handed down. If you were a poet, as you say, you wouldn't have tempted history with your campaign in Italy, you wouldn't have tempted it with the dart. It is hope that preserves life, not fear. Fear only preserves survival. You wanted to preserve art historically when poetry preserves history artistically. And what have you achieved? Losing the classical world and your love, what you wanted to preserve and what you believed you had started. You have fallen into what you intended to avoid, and you have behaved barbarously, instinctively."

"It was a dream . . . one night . . ."

"No, none of that. It was an illusion, a curved acceleration between your precedence and your incidence. It was what it still is, not a night, a reflectionless morning."

Quixote stills his head. From his knees, his hands hang over his shins like two gloves, turned inside out and therefore bunched. The index fingers appear to want to point at the toe on the same side, and the thumbs to stamp the one opposite.

"I'm thirsty," he says, standing as he moves down the dune toward the spring.

The other side of the trunk is melaphyre. And filaments sense the atmospheric water. The exaggerated air runs over them, without discontinuing it, like beads of light, crowned and snub. Toward the dune toward the melaphyre both, the filaments form corners without twisting, and oarsman and helmsman flutter, the water and the air, earth between fires. "What floats, did it rise or sink? the fluid in another fluid, which direction does it give and which does it take?" thinks Hydattila, making flourishes with the tip of his foot in the sand, neither dulled by dust nor dulled by sun.

The flower is worth the air, the granite the water, the glass the earth and "what is fire worth?" Hydattila says. "Granitic and flowered glass?" He thinks. "Of course . . ." and thinks "iris."

"I take your word!"

"But I wasn't saying anything," Ipsibidimidiata answers Attila. And senses Hydattila on the other side of the porphyry trunk.

"And what were you hearing?" Attila asks her.

"A strange trill. Why do I say strange? I found it immediately familiar. I stopped remembering, and without representing myself or imagining anything I felt a . . . stinging . . . urge to start writing . . . I was going to say a poem but I don't know if that was it . . . To write . . . but no word, neither found nor sought . . . comes . . . when you startled me, with your . . ."

"Well?"

Ipsibidimidiata shakes her head. She looks at Hydattila, face somewhat lowered, with increasing fixity, but more relaxed at the same time. "Who is he?"

"You ask it of me?"

"Like a bit ago, that language-less time, this nameless recognition, the wild urge to . . . to . . ."

"To locate."

"Yes, but what? but who? and where?" Attila feigns distraction.

Ipsibidimidiata motions at Hydattila, now watching her, to move away from the trunk, first to one side, and then to the other, so quickly that he takes it as a sign that he should disappear.

He moves to the side that takes him farther from her, "in part of some step I glimpse you. Path of exaggeration, perfection of the flaw."

Ipsibidimidiata raises her eyebrows.

"Oriental courtship. The man is seated behind the courted woman and addresses her friend who is in front of her," Hydattila weighs mentally. "Art will be less and less beautiful," he blurts to Ipsibidimidiata, who bends her head as she pulls back her chin and looks at him sarcastically: He holds back the smile from his lips but not his eyes and silences several yeses. "Will be, will be, will be," she says, accentuating the e's. "Less beautiful."

"The neverending story."

"Is the alwaysbeginning story," Hydattila pieces together.

"But beauty . . . bridges love and death . . . !"

". . . for being the myth of art . . ." Silence.

"Where are we?"

"My understanding is that I cannot tell you if I don't know who you are."

"And you can't know who he is knowing only who he has been," thinks Attila.

"I love you."

Ipsibidimidiata laughs in rivulets. "That doesn't tell me who you are."

"But it's what I most am now!"

"At what time?" Attila interjects.

Hydattila scowls but that doesn't stop him from observing that he is under a cloudless and sunless sky, luminous with no focus.

"At what time were you talking about beauty and what was then what you were most?"

Ipsibidimidiata places the palms of her fingers to her lips so he won't hear her laugh, and chokes on the tip of the cordial "beauty."

A haloed blush of a dawning green shines through Hydattila's cheeks. "I wasn't talking about beauty itself," he protests.

"Nothing in itself. You were taking a risk, all." Attila bends the trunk. "But who will credit it?"

"My person."

"You say you are what you say and you say what is not yet."

"I've said that I love you." Hydattila gestures impatiently with his elbow, followed by his torso.

"In effect. You love in the present and court in the future. How is that?"

Ipsibidimidiata nibbles her thumbnail between her second incisors, and the whites of her eyes glint around pinpoint pupils.

"The best was present in my mind."

"If you always do the same thing, you must have all the worst in the past."

"I have nothing in the past," Hydattila replies, annoyed.

"Then the worst has you."

"I will not bear this insolence!"

Ipsibidimidiata stands with her hands at elbow height.

"As you wish. But its pertinence bears you already."

"What is there to reproach me for?"

"You to you, or the worst to you?

"I demand an explanation!"

"Demand an understanding, if you think it sensible. I will only explain to you what I need."

Hydattila looks at Attila with exaggerated eyes.

"Me, serve?" he thinks.

Divinely inspired and autogenous, be gone! Attila thinks. "And nothing to thank you for, is that right?" he says.

"Yes, everything, in perfection, the future."

"Ah, lord with no teacher, lord ascendant of his descendants?"

"Never! but there is much I've had to unlearn, that is, lower a lot of ascendency."

"Blah, blah, blah, aba! If you sift a handful of this sand from one hand to the other and hear its account, perhaps you will know how much that is, and it will hear you."

In Ipsibidimidiata's pinheads, Attila's admonition is a burning lens.

Unicurved angels among beseeching curveback men. Angels unallied by desiring to be born and sexed by desiring to know. Angels silvered in feathered men for not desiring to die. Atlan angels beneath the proverbial man, crawling over the butchered man. The angel of the folds, stranger to the summary. Quarterer of the trivial trace. Neverender. Angel of breakage who keeps watch with the mouth. With wings in skid, and eyes in abundance. The cephalopterus perched in the armpit. Climber of chasm. Uncuttable pineapple, untotalizable bunch, the god's sense of hearing and smell. Tangled membrane. The counterfoil of the orb. Angel without original survivor, tongue conceived in the lacrimal horn. Excessively early for not being tardy enough. Angel of art, circling the back. Titan's tactile marrow. Mouse between man and angel. Scalloped trace of a banister, without balustrades. Squeezing unfocus, juicing disdain. Angel with the concave shape, heating another front. Platyrrhines in the kiss. All of Nature is the angel's great wing, with fire joints and air pinion.

Laocoön's sodden voice crosses the dune: "What use is your talent for finding out what has happened if nothing can be prevented?"

"Yes, nothing can be foreseen. For finding out the causes can prevent the effects. Besides, it allows for what has happened to be the glory of my present, and for that glory not to pass. It allows it to survive my responsibility."

"It doesn't allow it to survive mine," laughing seriously Laocoön goes back to speaking to Solomon. "So what has happened is the glory of your present . . . and furthermore that glory doesn't pass. Glory of two whores."

"It's worth more than the glory of two snakes. Did you happen to see them coming?"

"Boae coiled left to right, like an embryo, in the direction in which entrails turn, and Periboea coiled right to left. Your talent cannot prevent the effects if it can't prevent the causes. It passes through nothing, it only verifies what passes through it. Distrust a gift of correct answers that can only hit upon errors."

"And what else does yours foresee? . . . and what glory does your present have? . . . because glory is not the reflection of truth, but only the faith in recognition . . . Everyone prefers to recognize themselves in a past of whores than in a future of snakes . . . in a prostituted ancestry rather than in a slithering descendant."

"Yes. The bad listeners will be cursers . . . because the bad listeners were liars," Solomon joins Laocoön.

The chromatic scale of a melismatic "yes" followed by a "fu" to those voices comes from the indigo trunk.

Laocoön says: "and after a son?"

"Sleep. After coupling."

"After giving birth."

And now the athetosic voices of Melantho and Living Son of a Bitch cross the dune toward the trunks. "How did you kill your homonym," the first one asks.

"Sh out ing."

"Ikil ldan tifasjus keyp ingim qui et."

"From me."

"Thei wan tedfyu chure."

"Mea past."

"Miefath ersh ou tedm ore."

"Meor dad imore."

The chromatic scale of a melismatic "bla" followed by that of a "ron" comes from the indigo trunk.

"What part of speech are the dead?" Antigone's voice comes over, operculated. "Only the parts with no divisor? Only speech that cannot be contradicted?"

"Ask Sheba," Laocoön replies.

Solomon interjects, "Neither the part that doesn't change, nor the part that transforms. The dead are a part of speech to which those ones, and reality, adapt, both the signified already and the yet to be signified. And that part affects all language."

"How can reality adapt to language?"

"Because nothing behaves without it. Life without language is deported."

Sheba asks, "To where?"

And it is Laocoön who answers, "To the future."

"With a turned back, the cherub guards the exit from Eden . . ."

". . . against the silence, a word between the smile of a babe in arms and the smile of the old man on a bench," Antigone joins Sheba.

The voices hear the chromatic scale of a melismatic "tin."

"The fruits of the tree of life make no noise when they fall," one of them thinks.

"Invex cryptasm of pressing absence that converts the edges of the integral cavity that fingerstall print and its negligible edge of one in my skin and in my mucous in my membrane and guts in my gums and my tailbone implicitly key in my conscience in a syndactyl layering of bellows that pant bellows that pulse bellows that tune the fork the transflection of a mirror so black the speculation of such dark ink perjetting reality launching reality through sackless bottoms despite the January divorce between the thing and its trace between the extensive and appearing thing and the intensive and cryptosmagorical trace that presses its relief low in reason unpadronating it between the back of the object and the back of the subject, that inflated turn around a fold that neither tunes nor pulses nor pants that does not open hollow whose virtue is to be unaffectable whose virtue is not being virtual squeezing my body in my conscience subtracting body from my body and adding body to my conscience a aaaaah why haven't I said ay? who said ah? haven't I said ach?

how the images flee like radioless vesper bats through the making of maps how the words flow through the dunes in a glass! And what am I doing that I unfold into limbs just quadruped now and fourhanded, could it be diplopia because of strabismic convergence? could it be that fear of pain is fear of mutilation, rostral, facial, or sexual? fusion of the trunk and head with their unfoldable reumbilication disjointing of each hand and foot which is mine who is me without being able to put the hand on the chest and with feet in lunel and that acceleration of panting and pulsing toward the tuning fork but not centripetal like with pain but centrifugal acceleration that buries me that presses us against the earth feet and hands but the tuning fork does not accelerate nor approach the unaffectable fold but that acceleration substracts conscience from—well! haven't I said wow? who said well? what am I doing that recomposite that exposed composite and reposite that gutting who I laugh at my fear and my pain no but it isn't like that who I laugh at my fear and who fear I laugh at my pain who sees double and who makes the fear and pain see double out of themselves and out of myself to myself I subject of myself and I slave to my subject my fear subject to whom me and my pain slave to my fear ah! oh! wow! is who I alcohol that only anesthetizes the fear separating the fusion of trunk and head with their uncreasables this that alienates pain that distracts it that unhinges it from the rhythms another's pain and less than other yes pain I other and less than I incompletely gutted," Quixote excavates the dune opening a tunnel.

———

In love how the pain of the spirit precedes that of the body that pain of the spirit that fumigates except the cerberin death so that the body's pain passes unscathed as problematically penetrable is man's brain as woman's sex and when the object does not keep its shadow at its base but on its face like that trunk in its melaphyric "I ask you what house can expect the peregrine rhythm, that of which all postcede?" What case of things is it "if each thing keeps in time with its otherness" if one thing is not the rhythm of all its cases and if the sand is more crusted by air than the foam, and that air is more crusted from water than in the mist "despite the celestial sand imparting the earth" don't you see? don't you see? don't you touch anything straight? "what present does that ventured pain have in this futurarium? that ventured pain in this futurarium?" what sifts the earth of man? what sieves the earth of woman? "how much and so much?" ventured in this one even though no one asks what shakes the melaphyre "shadow granules."

"We both need pain, while we are each satisfied if the other doesn't suffer," says Ipsibidimidiata to Hydattila.

"For now," Hydattila thinks out loud.

"Yes. Our need for pain is only . . . how shall I say . . . novice . . . rudimentary . . . no . . . inaugural."

"I don't know," he tells her. "But perhaps one day it won't be enough for the other not to suffer."

"Why should we keep needing pain? And, if not that sufficiency, what would be the fee for our service?"

Silence. "Doesn't it seem strange to you that there are no animals in this desert? That no life comes to the oasis?"

"It's still day. Wait until night falls . . ."

"What is that still?"

Ipsibidimidiata looks at the sky. The sand runs from Hydattila's fist to palm. Penetration is not an attribute of frequency rather frequency is a trait of penetration, in the same and general way that, how shall she put it, it is taken for granted, yes, how much of its state is passage, and so the earth's rhythm is, already, and not between still yes and still no, in the rhythm of water, that which passes, in frequency, through the rhythm of the earth, and is, already, the rhythm of air.

Inverted, half a lemniscate spins in the sky. Hydattila looks at the belly of Ipsibidimidiata's two eyes.

"You don't feel the acceleration, do you?" he speaks again.

Ipsibidimidiata shakes her head and "but I feel the rest . . ."

"At great speed."

Silence. And consideration of him on her part, "but that pain too . . . does not threaten the origin if you are with me . . . and moreover if I feel myself with you, something transfigures in it a certain excessive health . . . excessive disproportion . . . but not disproportionate excess, you understand? . . . as if the origin and your company determined the direction of that speed, and my company and that transcendence of health accounted, separately, for its meaning . . . In pain . . . like I am called Ipsibidimidiata . . ."

"Like you are called Ipsibidimidiata, period. Who else calls you that?"

In a low voice, "my father . . ."

"Attila."

". . . and . . ." silence. Perplexed, Ipsibidimidiata looks at Hydattila.

"You are called Ipsibidimidiata as if the pulse of hands divided when splitting water, or the breath of words on breaking the breath, or the tenor of feet when walking. I don't know how Attila or anyone else calls you Ipsibidimidiata. But I call you Ipsibidimidiata, my love, as if the pulse of hands did not divide when splitting water, nor the breath of words when breaking the breath, nor the tenor of feet when taking steps . . ."

"As a man does not separate the girl from the mother, nor does the boy separate the woman from the mother," she adds.

"Who calls you that?"

"My father and . . . my . . ."

"Mother," he thinks without saying it.

". . . your . . ."

He waits in anticipation.

As does she. "Your . . . !"

He thinks he hears "you." He mutters, "Attila and . . . ?"

". . . his . . ."

". . . me and his?" he thinks.

From the auricular seedbed, seminary glyph of axis, meristematic axil of a drooping branch, the racemose prefixed folds, unrecognizable transfers, quarter profiles for the figure of a face, dream lures between both sentinels, prelusive impacts in the first scene, of what's seen already what will be said, and what's heard already what will be seen, graft on limbs of objects, subject in pure objectal freedom of the dream, solely and always aliquotly objectified.

Not in vain does the foot join the ear, foot of the head, the sole with the spiral, the heel with the lobe, bells with the same tone. For the face is so good, so made for the sky as for the earth. Hence Isis's monocular veil. The mantle draped with dawn. The air, the monoclinic sylph.

"This love that I re—. . . feel incipient every time I see you, and that suffocates the development of the love that started the last time, makes me continue in distress, in loving you. How will I become your woman . . . if it fails, this love of mine, to be?"

"Don't worry. Every time I see you, I feel that I love you for the second time, always from the one previous, and I don't know how that is. I don't remember the first time, I can't remember it, as if I had embarked on a love of journeying, in motion . . . and the strangest thing, and the strangest thing would be for it to develop as I returned . . . back . . . from where . . . I don't know."

Ipsibidimidiata's eyes bulge erect until they gleam, crowned and halfway between the irises and the corners. A tear in inverted "t" from the girl's gleaming counterpoints.

Acidic saliva keels Hydattila's tongue.

They look at each other, like a heliotrope at the world's end and the exact point where the sun will rise.

"But what beginning . . ."

"The one that crosses . . ."

". . . will it be . . . ?"

". . . with . . ."

" . . . "

" . . . "

———

And how inebriated fear laughs at whosoever suffers it how inebriated fear laughs at whosoever suffers pain and fear and inebriation for no anesthesia is perfect nor reconstituting nor even restituting and laughter is the only thought that perpenetrates the anesthesia and how the national anthem of the aged flattens the sharpened nativity carol of the easter politicians and inebriation itself how it exaggerates the mutism of the one pain making it exaggerated and exagent and exactive until being rehabilitated adept and inebriated fear how brave it feels and how it mocks the fear the one in pain shows it and the pain how it appeals to inebriation to avenge itself and inebriation how it gives for greater dilation of its vanity summoning its generator and granting resources to its nominator. "What have you let happen to my children in Monipodio's courtyard, enclosed within interminable walls, sat on the scaffolds of angels astride gargoyles in disrepair, leaving them such a strip of sky that in it every star seems shooting what have you let happen to my daughters in the adventitious streets why do they carry on their faces the breaking colors of the liver and the heart of bile and guts what have you let happen to my things giving them up, neglected, sidetracked, predestining them to a common void what have you let happen to my works disjoining them from the earth what have you let be said with my words at the city gates why do they lack no scale though they still have thorns?"

"Bah!" the indigo trunk instills in Quixote. Does memory marry better with harm than with alcohol and thus the recollection forgets them the omphaloskepsis that becomes every binge the remanence in derivation of the same that cannot be said in two languages the weeping that precedes the first dream the omphaloskepsis that every binge becomes the ballast of hope the Trojan gift that is every work of art? what sticks hope's rump to the bottom of the box what resonates in the cellar of every poem oh."

Dawn's ablative cheeping?

"... ha ha ha ha ..."

O dawn's ablative cheeping!

Ha h.

fv fv fv fv fv fv fv

"How is it. How is it that the dead see me when they look backward. Looking at me they go back," says the voice of Solomon, of Living Son of a Bitch, of Melantho, "to looking so young so adolescenting of presentaneous seat, being in the place of my senescence. And since all of their eyes are the same, the thing is they expound the citation of that gaze, the indefensible dedication tomorrow of my instant image. And how is that they do not demand my death, nor avenge that I am not dead, but my life, which is not sufficiently alive for them, if not but for them. Making so my life avenges that it is not grown, my age demanding of its own survival."

fv

"In the palantine nave, their common tongue, unbridled by frenulum, slips in deep, as if what happens with the canvases happens with them, and in their inversion they lose the excess means, since upright they retain the missing means, the ends, in a word. That this tongue seems so desirable, so in a living place, absolver of my erostratism," say the voices of the Living Son of a Bitch, Melantho, and Solomon.

"As if death were also a question of language, a paraword, arising before the first syllable, the first syllable with a vowel, a question of another orality, placed before either gets away with it."

No hope sustains the angel. No angel is held by faith. Nor from love does any angel hang.

The air contracts. It doesn't condense. It airs itself. It withdraws from all borders, liquid, solid. The air is its own border. Against itself it conspires with itself. With itself it conspires against itself. In time. Very slowly. In its time. Continuously. To the other. Time of the indigo trunk.

The water contracts. It doesn't condense. It washes itself. It withdraws from all borders, solid, gaseous. The water on its own border. Gravity is the piston of its lightness if its lightness is the cylinder of its gravity. And vice versa. Against itself it beats with itself. With itself it beats against itself. In the time. Slowly. In its time. Continuously. To the other. Time of the indigo trunk.

The earth contracts. It doesn't sublimate. It buries itself. It withdraws from all borders, gaseous, liquid. It withdraws from its objective and withdraws from its ocular, it corners itself and screams at its image. Its unperishing image of a perished past, interposed, rash and flattering, yet resigning from all fractures, between a subjunctive future of imperfection and the present of perfect perishability. Its oscillating and taunting image of its time in its time for its time.

Against itself it vibrates with itself. With itself it vibrates against itself. In time. Quickly. In its time. Contiguously. To the other. Time of the indigo trunk.

"Do not believe me, I'm estranged by death. For we are still all brothers of one origin. What do I care if you make a figure of me? If you become protagonists at my expense? As long as, for when?, today will be the day when it will be, today is the day that nothing returns, that does not admit return, in what time?, as long as, are you now at my expense?, now, but here?, here will be the place where there will be there, here will be the place where there is, here is the place from which nothing goes, that does not admit departure, end of the barbaric foreshortening of the border, end of the slighted insult, ours for being for little, where not repeated by when, how confraternized, the how telagonistic, may you be undelegates for life!"

Neither Laocoön, nor Antigone, nor Sheba hear the voice of the Specter of Absalom.

"Solomon is no longer sure of dying," says Laocoön.

"Not even of that," adds Antigone.

"Not even he . . ." Sheba interjects.

". . . what will become of . . ." Antigone joins.

". . . much less the others," Sheba concludes.

"He doesn't feel guilty," the paroxytone, Laocoön,

"They feel responsible," the oxytone, Antigone,

"For being able to die," Sheba mediates.

"And for not being able to die," Antigone adds.

———

Above and behind Attila the sky yellows, blues, and reddens, not in the way of twilight, in skeins and loose threads, but very clearly, in inlays of ovals and lobes, cupped by the delicate canopy of a capital tree. Hydattila and Ipsibidimidiata see that sky, but the one above and behind them, watched by Attila, blues airily in catenary series of irregular squares, a battery of series whose edge reddens watery, and each trapezoidal series yellows earthily at its edges, diffusely raining soil from the bosom of the sky, and water fusely from its orb.

Between them and Attila the indigo trunk drips redly under a sky that bitterly expels what it bluely sifts, its amorphia.

Quixote's dune includes blue glass, and between it and the red panes that the sky concludes stretches the beadwork where enormous red carp swim, omnicovex and anomalous, and between it and the crystalline beat of the sky's red conclusion stretches the turbid and glaucescent blue in which the carps' green shadows float, and the red pulse does not stretch between the yellow tremolo and sky's blue breath allowing the Specter of Absalom's retruded rhythms to emerge in coordination, coordinating, coordinating and allowing the fourth trunk, the square one, to not only appositively juxtapose the interrupted sequence of pure measures, not only rhythmically intercross the same interrupted sequence but interrupt them all, revealing the red rhythmic essence of blue, and the yellow rhythmic essence of red, revealing Thalia's yellow.

Hydattila drops the handful of sand. "It isn't something in the past, it is something in the present that history instigates," he thinks.

The double is not double for nothing but for the same. The double is not double for nobody, but for oneself, Attila rethinks.

It isn't something in the present, it is something in the future that embroils utopia.

"How to reside in a dune? how to shape the main piece furniture? how to suffer without stamping? and anesthetize without alertness, a pain refounded in the refuge, in the fleeing depths of its work, merely touchable by entelechy, how to turn up in a nightmare? how to correct the tangent blot that dissects the line? how not to get drunk, until fear gives itself the scare of a century, of the whole world, and anesthesia hurts, the whole embedded in its heaviest part, subventure, tectonically, architectonically raising the future?"

"And, naturally, only, all your verbs only, naturally all your verbs only," Attila interrupts Quixote's monologue. "What is Ipsibidimidiata's place in them? Or perhaps you mean to frighten her? And what place in them is left unoccupied by the Specter of Absalom? Do you both fit? Or perhaps you mean to get him drunk?"

"Get a ghost drunk . . ." Quixote repeats, thoughtful and smiling. "The first pain's last binge . . . the last binge for the first pain."

"How could you not urge him to seek revenge? In your dreams, in your melopoeia. Let him be."

"Say instead: let him follow . . . come in second . . . let him follow you." Quixote relaxes his smile and shrugs the shoulder on the side he faces. "In any case, the addition of vindication is the peel of presence. What does it matter to me? What can it matter, whether I let him be or not."

Silence. "And Ipsibidimidiata, how?"

A yellow tear appears, grains of sand in its belly.

"With art?"

"The perfection of the work is not the art, it is the action," and Quixote's eyelids rattle his tarsi ". . . and this is why, only because of the pain of the living and the specters, only because of this, this is why each one's head is not only the head of each . . . and why Ipsibidimidiata . . ."

"And that you!? . . . Besides . . . it is not solely for that . . ." and Attila's eyebrows look like two crows in a squall.

"No one who still doesn't know that a word devours itself knows anything." Quixote shakes his head, as if it were a basket for draining greens.

"What rhythm can . . . curl the curl . . . among . . ."

Around Thalia's trunk, holding hands, Hydattila and Ipsibidimidiata sit.

Quixote exits the dune and heads toward Hydattila, who turns his back to him.

The four arms appear to rest on one crow's nest, and their chins on another. From their cranial domes, blind consciousness oozes. From the palatal dome that consciousness spurts, transparent, sameable, penetrated by a point, seen by a point, the consciousness of black father and yellow mother, science with the transparent color of fire, the geophanous color of fire, with no knowledge of cause, with no knowledge of concept, with knowledge of knowledge, and another crow's nest appears to rest over their heads.

In the fifth trunk, the perforated trunk, the voices of Solomon and Laocoön and Living Son of a Bitch and Melantho and Sheba and Antigone converge, converge tightly squeezed, and squeeze and shrink as they pass through the foramen in a yawning melisma.

It is the feet the sand sways, not intoxication "and all the fear of history brought to light in the incorporable hiatus, the procession, which cannot be reduced, of one's own childhood, for then indeed each one was his brother, only that and only then, and that the reflex had more, all, importance than the influx," it's not the intoxication "and all the fear of history in the hiatus of expression, the dry dock of the image in the plurality with neither cardinals nor ordinals, quantumly vocative, the mandatorily graphic hiatus between the symbol of what sees, touches, and speaks, and the impenetrable hollowness of the class." A barely tilted red line crosses the low sky, breaks, cuts the horizon and in parallel crosses the high earth "dynastology" would be the drain word, if ". . . it could be reversed," Quixote reformulates, "if it could be reversed: what is watched over by heroes with rhombic torches, plundered by poets" . . . the eroded treasure of the pandynastic landfill, loses once again.

"There is something new underground," Hydattila says to himself.

"Artificial life . . . because artificial isn't opposed to mortal. My back is frozen. The living artifice . . . because living it opposes the mortal. The dead don't have feet. And meanwhile . . . that anticipation of life with its chariot games . . . of delayed death, that woodworm of the book of propagated survival, of propagation survived, monostome and monodactylus cyclops that eats through its eye and sees through its finger. I feel on one foot what the other foot expels, and that's how they walk, fending off the other's expulsion like two yoked ships. The meantime . . . registered only in the as yet, totally, for now, swirling along the side of a current that boils near its bottom, from its light to what the dead thumbs point to, what was not done, the parallelism of the heavens."

Ipsibidimidiata doesn't hear Quixote either, and says to herself "fingers are to the skull what the face is to the palm." She opens her eyes and sees Hydattila's head emerging from the head of Hydattila.

"morviraggratammoria"

"And all the difficulty, all the difficulty of the spectral world is in the indication, how to deal with space . . . infinitive. Without shifting the commandments, processes, shares, desires, and possibilities . . . How to shortcut, bypass, the work of art . . . without dislocating objective language, disarticulating the natural school until water, stone, and air get along, how, without violence of word and thing, short-circuit parable and case, how to get out of the theater without getting out of everything, and enter into nothing, how to get out of sight, that is to say person and scene, without getting out of the act. How to do the miracle without undoing something . . . without causing surprise, but recognition . . . without saying, for example, 'gulfarutio.'"

"Why do you respect the desinence?" Melantho asks the Specter of Absalom, unraveling herself from the melisma.

"Without beating the skin impotently around the crowds who walking backward do not see that they lease their origin, the skin around the most promising place, therefore," the voice of Antigone replies, sallying forth.

A graft in the shape of a shield shines on the night indigo trunk.

Ipsibidimidiata sees the head of Quixote swallowing Quixote's head and releases her hands when she sees Quixote's swallowed head in his stomach.

"...the garden of sapient stones and its adaptable plants..." Sheba says as she arrives and is cut off.

"Fatigue doesn't wander aimlessly because obstinacy doesn't ride, and at the forefront the hooded cattle don't set their feet on the ground in chaos and noiseless fury, frontal eyes of all of them, steadfast by any of them, the quadrupeds also have their angels given that they can only die before the goaded ground and not scrabbling out of the dirt, in the land of nothing, fireless land of a waterless air..."

"The lovers' garden," Sheba's voice resumes, "bulges lethally," cutting off the Specter of Absalom.

"One has what the one seeks, and another has what both seek," adds and embellishes the voice of Living Son of a Bitch.

From Ipsibidimidiata's forehead her profile hangs, and Quixote doesn't see the auricular scallop or the nasal fillet, just the undulating tapestry and its sculpted shadows through a rearward and crossed spotlight, travelers of serialized permanence escorting and serializing it simultaneously.

With "the half profile is better for judgement" Solomon's voice carries the wrapped voice of Laocoön, who continues ". . . the whole body, do you hear me? the whole body is soul, and every limb, do you hear? every limb is all soul. But only those of men are . . ."

"What does that matter if their eyes are pantographs like those of women?" Solomon's voice interferes again.

Hydattila's are closed still.

"In a triangle."

"With a set square. Women sell their bodies . . ."

". . . because men sell their souls," finishes Laocoön.

One must always write as if one could not write. Ipsibidimidiata thinks, but her consciousness doesn't insert that assertion, nor does Quixote's vision, but with open eyes she remains in her geophany, as does Hydattila in his, each in their fire that burns through earth and water and air without ustion, their ovoid fire, and peeling fire, fire suspended of itself, and suspensive of the elements, eager for another combustible . . . and meanwhile, harmonizing the triple rhythm, consonant of consonants, amid so much house without walls or windows, without foundations or furniture, paranimphic, nuptial, the house of being mute and of changing state, and aedicule of all space exposed to weather and open to the sky, which no division takes by storm, healer of physical space and temple of atomic time . . .

"Between the vinegar of the imperfect future and the salt of the perfect past . . . love comes, and inevitably we betray the past perfection, it comes at dusk and doesn't finish coming until dawn, and it witnesses us with backs in salt and feet in brine . . ." Quixote says, constant in his contemplation of Ipsibidimidiata.

"The days' light is engraved in the mud of tomorrow, and there are pasts that are yet the future of a past, and all futures are today's past, and there are no days of overlap, there's no overlap of days, there's only inclusion, in the lesser past."

"And the last dusk will be today's dawn," Quixote answers the Specter of Absalom, but without turning toward the indigo trunk, resting, instead, his gaze on the back of Hydattila's skull.

"The adjustment of all ruins. Adjustment of ruins. Of all of them. Of each with all the others. Including that natural history is the ruin of human history. And yet any verbal form is the ruin of the plastic form. A plastic. For action is today's ruin. And today is the ruin of here. Day. Without night. Solar ruin. Appearing after dawn and consummated before sunset. Midday reminding the half day that history is supreme, and, as such, vertical. Nodding figureheads. In the harbor. Each ruin has been salian and will have been shielded. Art is the craftsmanship of ruin. The production that ruins the present so it does not become absent. The product nonconducting to the step. Only to the leap. Each ruin is a settling ring. And only a leap can settle all the ruins. Including that any verbal form is ruinous paternity. And yet the plastic ruin is affiliated. The ruinous filial form. Because the origin is the end's ruin. And the end is the ruin of nothingness. Nocturnal ruin. Art revealing to beauty that flaw is essence, and, as such, incapable of repetition. Rhythm without iteration. Son revealing to the father that essence is demon, and, as such, incapable of being avoided. That essence is also plural. Where the sword that will have crossed the staff has been. Every ruin is armed peace. The ruin revealing to beauty's clear identity the dark alterity of art. Revealing the son's ambiguous altruism to the father's univocal selfishness. Only a sheathed leap can adjust all the ruins. Including the indigenous ghosts, aboriginal and settler. And nomads of the newest. From the first reluctance of the latest. Because fashion is the ruin of novelty. And novelty is the ruin of exclusivity. Fresh. Ruin at first light. Without evenings. Misting the birth and fogging the death. The voice of he who is born and the light of he who dies. Piston of lubrication. Every ruin will have been filter and visor. All ghost is the child's ruin. A wing is the angel's ruin. That of blood and milk. And only rowing with the whetstone can he take the leap. But only a half leap. Excluding the ruin of the lovers. The master ruin. The least ministerial. The ugliest ruin. The totally worthless. And yet. For the half is the ruin of the double. And the double is the ruin of the whole. Ruin at the edge of night. With stones over flowers. Aphyllous garden. With stones over flowers. Disfiguring the idols and mourning the simulacrum. Echo of strangers. Each ruin will also be the lovers' ruin. Love is the ruin's mystic limb. The segment between its perfection and its completion. Ruin is the only timely anticipation. And only a leap from the void can settle all the ruins," cries Attila and cries the landscape without coordinated hours, the waters of its raked sand, the mosaics of its serrated air, and its cuckolded pool downwind from the dune, and the Chinese lanterns of its stars on all fours.

VII

DOUBLE BY DAY AND HUN BY NIGHT

It will be the oldest profession in the world
If the oldest profession in the world
Continues to be attributed to the red man
Like the foulest moment is to air.
Like the least worldly minute in the sky
The encounter between the lame man
And the thick-lipped woman in the loose passage
Will be protested if asserted roundly.
A slap for each corner
And two for the opposite wall?
Whoever crosses the street crosses the face
Whoever uncrosses it walls the ruin.
He who enters will stay silent if he doesn't lie
But he who stays silent won't leave indifferent.
If the profession of the long-winded elder
Continues to inherit the reflex verb,
Patrimony of the prudish youth

The profession of the pair will be complex,
Like the one who is unparalleled will be barren
Like the unparalleled plunder is done.
Ancient traffic of hyaline light
Will the encounter be blushing?
Between stream and lubricating gutter.
Every decline is a pilgrim
If with courage it cradles its debris
In every hospital in every valley,
Respective hospitals of mutual valley
Behind shrine and before curtain.
The one who enters will stay silent if he doesn't lie
But who stays silent will not leave indifferent.

As if it were missing two transmission legs, so long would
be the mount, and its shadow would mold to the terrain, so
that in some places it would appear foreshortened, as if the
mount had extra arms. Transmission legs that would have
lengthened Quixote's own, the effect all the more ampu-
tating because those legs would be armed with tibia and
fibula, and the instep of each foot with tarsi and metatarsi,
the end of a suit of armor that would protect the knee with
a cap and with a femur the outer thigh, a pelvic bone for
each hip, fastened at the sacrum and pubis, back with verte-
brae and sides with ribs, the chest after a sternum, and the
throat protected by a hinged jaw, the head, the arms, and the
hands by their respective bones of a skeleton all belonging
to Quixote, but instantly sculpted over. Like bearded fish,
the mountains would stir the sand, squirming in the clouds

to remain in the desert, and some ranges, like congers and morays, undulating chiaroscuros, their axial plane not always on the plumb line. On the other hand, the mount's mane was longer than the bristles of its tail, somewhere else its shadow would be Quixote's squire. The one eye of the underground river would be obstructed once the paved parts appeared elsewhere.

Quixote will advance anticlinally toward the Celestial Empire. He will have even advanced synclinally. Behind, the druse will have smoked, and the apex of the cloud will fall back like a Phrygian cap.

Luoyang's walls will look like festoons when the thousand stupas, pagodas, and monasteries are finished being built. Its orthogonal streets will not run parallel to the walls but the four walls will project from the imperial enclosure, the emperor's choices and tastes intertwining, six-story pagodas with their diamond cornices and varied finishes, the most luxurious brothels in the empire, which will entice with their prominent corbels, golden, red, and green, taverns with more doors than windows, monasteries with uneven roofs, workshops of fine craftsmanship, temples, and manor houses. Luoyang's splendid walls would have seemed mere dikes of the Kien and Luo rivers.

Quixote will leave the Temple of the White Horse on his left back when in dust it will have bathed Pegasus, and he will enter the city through one of its western gates. Hundreds of garments in trapezoids and cylinders will mend the geometric void, and a network of noises and sounds will offset natural time. The Pagoda of Eternal Peace would have been on his right when he arrives at Luoyang's main artery, and he will see to the north of the crossroads the main entrance of the palace enclosure and to the south the river's uneven shore. The two corners opposite will put in relief some noble's wealthy home and a refined inn.

He will be savoring the bain-marie dumplings and rice wine when he sees a serving woman in a doorframe, dressed in a long pluri-plaited skirt the color of amber, and a cherry blouse, cinched at the waist with a triple-looped ribbon, while from the wide sleeves an embroidered strip of the same cherry color hangs, gathering the widening of the skirt under and behind her calves as she walks. She would wear a high bun headpiece, held this way with strings of pearl that find their grip in the foremost part of the hair, leaving a fine, long strand free on each side, and enough hair to neatly cover the neck at the back. Like pelagic flowers, the hands will not show, but the blouse will have splattered the lips, forehead, and cheek—though not a Wei lady!—toward the servant, the profile would become Ipsibidimidiata.

Arms and back relaxed from the meal, his belly warmed by the rice wine, Quixote, feeling heat and swelling in his thighs, will be about to rise. Bow and horse he would leave at the inn.

The sword will hang to the right of his waist over the indigo tunic bordered with light chestnut, crossed over the chest and with gathered sleeves, when Quixote crosses the street to present himself at the neighboring mansion.

She would have been in front of the mirrored bronze oval, kneeling on the carpet in her loose dressing gown, touching up an eyebrow with her right hand held by a double bracelet and the stick held by the end of the thumb and the root of the index finger, having combed her hair again, this time with a two-tiered bun at the center of her head gathering in its skeins all the strands of her hair.

And hoarily, summer won't have known to ripen anything but distillable sugar and the straw-colored lascivious light of autumn, offering cold to melancholy so that it may impregnate the season.

On entering the dressing room, he would hear her recite the famous lines from Li Sao "it was the name the True Example gave me," looking at herself in the mirror in the beginning and at him at the end of the verse.

The entrance to the shell basket of the paper nautilus will look like the hem of her tunic and her leg like a snowy branch of an orange tree will pass over Quixote's shoulder. And her silky coralline vulva the balm and not a wound.

They would aerially bury the water and aqually the fire.

Injure. Mineral resonance of a formidable cry. That of a male.

Behind Ipsibidimidiata's half profile see the ruffled simian slurping the light from her face and leaving but a red rust the deepest hollows.

From the balcony, see the servant watching Quixote crossing the courtyard toward the door, heralded by the shadow of a horse stretching all the way to his soles.

Somewhere between their faces, she will remember Quixote's eyes, which would have swooped down on hers, floating frosted.

In that ultrafolded space.

The remains of the suicided mystics pass before Quixote, carried by a processional retinue that fills the street. "Perhaps health simply responds to the need to survive, since being alive means being able to be sick, and that's why suicide would correspond to both the extremes of pleasure and the extremes of pain. Why will those religions have entered into the world's cities? why will they open their doors to such unpolitical metaphysics? to govern the dominated cultures, or to govern the urban excesses of cruelty and debauchery? but what calculus is that? won't the redeeming doctrines bring with them idyllic orders contrary to the amassing of power? in which case the civilizations would produce an art without empire? what requirement is that? a city without a forum, or a civic suicide." The caudal remains of the procession pass before Quixote, and in the gaps he sees an old woman moving along the wall opposite, leaving the inn, and thinks, the indivisibility of love, which the preclinical passage of time does not allow to prove, could find reason in the old woman's debt, that the continent reflux, owing to simple inaptitude, of rostrality, its negligible asymmetry. Yes! that's it, the art of the paid-off cities return to rostrality, as it would have been in the times of archaic cities, prostituted, made available as the corner piece will have been for all time. An art for sickening, and for fearing, and for striving to survive. If these should be the times.

Cross the street and follow the old woman, intending to catch up to her, and give her a surprise. He will walk on the bias, his right arm raised out ahead as if clearing his way, and his hand upright to hide himself, pressed to the wall, and running for stretches, hunched. As if engaged in the wall by her eight-lobed bun, the old woman glides, and even her dress does not crease as she climbs two steps and enters the brothel.

He grabs her when she reaches the double-boarded console, one hand resting on a knee, the other on the ground and its homologous hand gripping the edge of the low table, where two jade panthers with horse tails and rhinoceros' horns between their ears, crouched in a circle, looked about to bite her long-nailed fingers. Lift her celadon tunic and loosen the waistbelt so the root of her thigh and leathery hyacinth sex won't be visible to the entire brothel. Run your right hand like a paperknife under the left lapel and gather the carob-like breasts by their long and twisted nipples while the left hand goes up through the bell of the skirt and seeks at its core the necessary moisture so that the smooth and impermeable bark won't run. Like a young lion, bite her crimped neck pulling her face up toward you until you see past the gray the lines on her forehead, crow's feet, wrinkles between cheek and lip and chin spilling black and cherry makeup on a young and confluent profile, soon to be ink-red all, indistinct from Ipsibidimidiata's.

The terracotta chimera will remain supported by its rhinoceros hands and its haunches, blue-gray with igneous eyes and tongue, three spikes on its back and a leonine mane, guarding the exit with its three steel teeth around wide jaws, guarding the passage, from the house of ill repute with its two shutters side by side but one more latticed than the other, behind the ground floor balconies, and its elegant dormered aedicule at the center of the roof, betrayed by the precedence of a horse's shadow.

From the window of his small hotel she contemplates the first fold with which the moon overtakes the sky and the earth, the sphincters of folds that are the stairs and the things that on earth, even jumping, never cease to be folds, all of them, he contemplates that universal transfolding, which suggests the thrust or now the aspiration of metaphysical labors on the other side, instantaneously blunt and eternally sharp, tasks for demiurgical hands with fingergloves embolized by their own ends, never secant maneuvers of animation and incorporation that turn the Luoyang cliffs into the exposure to its own defense from this night a filter suspended by the ridge, from the coming dawn the thin skin of the diurnal earth embroidered with words that dusk will vein, from the flag a ballast, from the recurrent pain the helm waters, from a lash the tiger, and from a love bite the nightmare, maneuvers of consignment and tangential causality always, every minimal variation setting back all rhythmic regeneration, the folds of water mounted in the folds of air, the folds of earth mounted in the folds of water, the folds of fire mounted in the folds of earth, and so the nocturnal sky becomes transparent, the suctorial unfolding, posting of phallic sphinxes, if he contemplates the first fold with which the moon tunes not to the harmony of the spheres but the consonance of the segments.

She turns her back to the window and Quixote removes her ornamental comb. "Be that as it may, the Chinese cities will have resisted the barbarian migrations, absorbing the energy of their cultures, and my brothers will achieve here what I cannot in Rome, the safeguarding of the classical empire. To be sure, between the Hunnic Xianbei and the cities, the vandal hordes would not interfere here. The exclusively tactical nature of my Western error will not have proven Attila's cultural strategy correct; rather, the current course of Chinese civilization would testify to my strategy. Here is what Attila should stop and think about, and what I should continue to do."

"Ars armatoria, bellum politicum, may that be the citizens' angular momentum."

Sharpen your mustaches and play a little with the bow at your double chin.

A Tibetan cat meows on polished roof tiles.

"Only outside the city does the dust not matter," and like before, he will pronounce some of the words.

She plays the seven silk strings without a pick and her long nails shine less than the recumbent and lacquered body of the qin. On entering the dimmed light of the luthier's open house, Quixote observes the socket's glossy subciliary protrusion, the cheekbone like a pomegranate's gold leaf over ripe fruit, and the button nose like an opal between the moons of its wings, the arranged black hair of the pubescent girl quietening on the rug and only then, and then only, the turned lip, heart-stopping pale.

The pliable silks reveal the untamperable plasticity of all furniture therein. And Quixote observes that around the eye the nose would overlap the face, and the face would overlap the temple. "What severity!" he would think and will mutter, linking with the verse from the Odes, "The sky does not jest with its severity," "the sweet flute ought to accompany it," and he will squat. The maimed simian's diminutive cry crosses the street and is enfolded by the qin. The palestral young girls seek each other in the immovable bodies, Quixote's body backlit and hers light-fugitive, and attend from the threshold to the middle of the street the shadow of a horse with a knotted tail. They pass over the patina of the burgundy rosewood table, and he glimpses, frosted by the hair at the earlobe, Ipsibidimidiata's profile.

He will walk backward out of the shop. And his equine shadow will penetrate the restaurant. He goes down the street, south side to the river, and avoids the market stable.

Recruiting units will stop the young men in the neighboring quarter, from whose enclosure the guards at the gate will stop any able-bodied man from escaping. Above it all, where a few half-buried houses will still survive, he will notice an out-of-bed bachelor gesturing goodbye to a young woman with no legs.

With an arm graceful yet strapping, round yet muscular, tendon fibers free-standing, she would spring the trap. And Quixote will follow her.

Against the sloping walls, like around the posts, there will appear funerary figurines, censers, cylindrical urns, yu stoneware cups, evocations of life and death invited by the fire to glaze their adornments. She would walk on her knuckles, swaying in the most reverberant air. She will climb onto a lathe. Quixote will have used it to undress her.

The buttocks, exact replicas of the breasts, tight, the little buttons faded in the light areolas, brace the haggard pubis, and draped over one shoulder, her hair will elongate the umbilical tilde. Quixote would make use of the lathe to caress her, keeping his lips and fingertips at fixed distances from the rotation. The crippled woman would have revealed herself to be the fountain woman, and he would gulp down the cyprine nectar, lifting her from the table by her elbows like an amphora.

Quixote will place himself on the lathe, his figure disappears between her arms crossed in an X, and he will sense until feeling and feel until knowing what she does, her ghostly limbs unveiled by pleasure, sprouting beyond the throat of the maiden, of the Ipsibidimidiatian profile.

Only the shadow of a horse's tail, haunches, and trunk would have remained outside the trap's roof. It would leave the potters' district darkened already by the falling night.

Folds of string that mark off apsaras, night sounds, signatories of the tapestry, desired skin that would have been the map of another woman, the mourning of the beloved to come early, desired skin the precursor of the grief of the other skin, sound of the skin that survives against the other skin that subsists, safe-passage through adverse times, them against the promise's old age, they pass through the stupid speeds of the opaque, contrary to the old age of the promise, through the luciferous mouthfuls, from what has been thus far, the remaining. Resignatories of the triple-fold wall hanging, on the sought-after ledges of the horizon, stopping in this way the wind of its horn, and the mother in another womb. From the white night departing from no surface, white on that side and on this side, and unsettled surface, like a paper's ashes on coals. Noises with muffler smelled, and tasted, tight-fitting inflamed. Night non. In the night non. In things inimitable for being so commissioned. For something. Congenitally broken inseparable. Steps, steps in the amphitheater of the earth, of the stars in the stands, notes in the lemniscogram. Sounds of perspiration and perlumination. From the plucked perspiration to the perluminated tuning fork. Sounds from the earth's interior and the exterior of the sky. Of defanged rays and bubbling drops. Night's thunderous gurgles.

"Let it be night and all light and let no one doubt the nictogenesis of all flame, for night is curved, and all light is the very curvature of the night. And let the night introduce itself in its curvature, let the sun be but one of its mere phantoms, just one of its self-portraits. Let no one doubt that the colors are night's iridescence, the changes in slope cone-up, for the night is enskirted in its conical hood and every color is the transient flaw of its unfolding, just the momentary alienation of its curvature. So let no one doubt that in the daze of vaginal night, all metempsychosis is rectified."

"Let night fall and let everyone, everyone be in its womb, and on the other side, from its inferred, induced convexity, let each one feel the souls' fetal movements, the soul fetuses' movements, on the other side, inferred, just inferred, and with tempting eyes search the universe for the end of the nocturnal curve, the eventide of the night that is not a dawn, the shored freedom of euthanasia, the melanangelic kiss."

"Let night fall and let the visible mystery be done, the entire curved visible mystery, let the mysterious curvature of everything sensible be made, the secretive binding of the tactile, the pensile division of the audible, the motored oscillation of the tasteable, and the spiral counterbalance of the scentable, the mysterious curvature of everything orientable, dented, embossed only by the insensible mystery. Of all that is dreamable, let dreams be the mere phantoms of the orientation.

"Let night fall and let the earth be on the tightest of its curve, on the ogive's snout, where man's witness does not unimmensely dilate woman, nor does the unimmensity of woman twinly constrict man, let the earth be through all the angles of the curve, supported only by the insensible mystery" but Quixote will have walked eastward and the day will dawn.

Inexplicably open and unguarded the north door of a domestic enclosure grants the eye and foot access to the garden. Entering on the right, after several steps the mountain of floured black flint would have hardly been seeking Luoyang's rocky outcrops more than the Ill-Fated Mountains and its tiered openings not only give to that arborescent shape and unusual cavern nativeness but moreover anticipate from the other side the small heraldic branches of the pomegranate tree beneath the black bamboo, the small white arch of the bridge in front of the waterfall, the serpentine blue of the conifer on the gray lake, and the sandy ochre before the small straw-colored tea room, the peach tree among the drowsy chrysanthemums, the orange tree's lascivious branches beneath the green bamboo, the steps converging in the jade pavilion, its luminous threshold, why on earth would I acknowledge recognition by Quixote "great is the creator, for he has made me deformed" from the Zhuangzi, his voluminous vestibule, tall yet temperate, his subsequent antechamber, the pedestal's lock keeper, cornice and base covered by another mineral carnality, aprons over skirts over hides of flesh, a cone of flaccid rings, not even relieved by the knees in lotus bloom, protected in the breasts, whose rear arches would be passing under the arms to find a grip beyond the shoulder blades, in the suspensory slice of the nape, a worker's body of an annexed solipsism, strangled asymptotically, chock-locked, knave-roofed, but the knees won't have been in lotus but kneecaps on the ground, and he, coated to the nose by the widest screw, spurred under her he will have felt his marrow drumming in his brain, the enclaving invagination of his bulb, the disengagement of his cranial bones. But not of his face. And when she gasps, when her air has burned and flesh unburdened in her pneumatolysis, the diagonal grooves, he will see in the soft diagonist the injured profile, or rather confronted by her ear, the helix of her same ear, with no room for doubt. Despite the monkey Ipsibidimidiata fits in a horse's skull.

———

Awaken Nature's lethal pilgrimage in the garden, the peregrine nature of death, the natural death of pilgrimage, eastern the death of the pilgrimage, principal the death of the pilgrimage, horizontal. Contemplate in the garden death's peregrine seed, its peregrine rudiments, the element's lethal pilgrimage, the omen's lethal pilgrimage, the initial omen, the morning omen of everything arboreal, the fowls and the monkeys, the most rostrate and the most platyrrhine, in the garden. And the laurel wreath made from a common woman for a common man. The formidable pressure it exerts. In love the physical world in the physical world and the metaphysical world in the metaphysical world. In death the physical world in the physical world and the metaphysical world in the metaphysical world. The mystical body of Eros and Thanatos. The physical garden mystically squeezed by the metaphysical garden. In the garden Nature would be being bodhisattvic. So that the final judgement has a place in the theater. So that only a comedy is judged. So that only a comedy is judged that night. It would be being bodhisattvic from its entire fellowship of cubs. From its entire cradle liking. And the lake dazzled by the drops. By the dazzling disparity. And the garden would remember what is presumed in yearning. The cephalic west of the born. Meloplastic place. Of death and of love. Marker of the rhythm. Tragicomic of desire. Let the hiding places be close and discoveries distant. Antidaedalus. For the fatal encounter. For the natural fate. For the deduplicate nature. For the unfolding unalienated for being misaligned. This is why Quixote will walk in the garden like the Dürer's knight between death and devil, he who only recognizes desire's tragic rhythm, the tragic rhythm of the lyric poet MacBeth, the rhythm of martial Eros, of damp uxoricidal Mars, the profile's phantasmagorical beat. "From the city he will go around the walls, wreaking havoc on his enemies," Quixote will foresay in the garden, and he will accomplish the ideal of truth: that the spring, winter's nymph, will have been autumn's most larval. See a monkey riding bareback on the withers of his galloping steed. So that in the garden the man is also the woman's death and vice versa. Locus festorum. Of love and of death. Of the woman-chalice and the anonymous man. In the garden Quixote will read the myth of the first time first, of the new woman new, as if it were a discovery at the origin, a gift at the origin, with no other alternative but the repetition of change.

The enormous challenge to human plicature, virile and feminine, keeping at bay waves of men, keeping at stiff bay storms of men, protagonists in all the agony of their gender, antagonists of all the genders of their agony. Taking the other folding by the other side of its fold, the feminine fold by the metaphysical side of its fold, the metaphysical world of its fold, immediately, fortunately, instantly, thus condemning itself to proceed with women by elimination, exhaustive. And with himself by trial and error.

And feel the proparoxytone beat of the gold leaves, the flat rhythm of the silvery cores and the acuteness of the bones under the tree of the forty shields.

Every garden, should it not be found in a grotto? With the gate in the theorem. The tree that castells the water and the rock. The monument staddle. The arborescent rock by the water arborified by the rock. The city naturalized in the subsoil. With the grotto gate at the garden's theorem. The subsoil, the climate's balm.

"They are seven days

And every seventh one, Caught on the gangue Of a single night" someone will recall of Quixote.

"And to continue,

The unique predicate

Be always everything," so they understand that "something held continues everything."

Trimmed with lace on the theorem, the compiled histories of a digression, or about the frequency with which the index finger would have wished to be the middle one, and the thumb would wish to be the index, and the middle be ringed in the opposable aura. Just as the possibility of the best would justify the alienation of the probable, so the best is mad because what is identical drives one mad. The movable soul, in the end, hospitalizing aedicules.

Horizontal gate so that the turbulences recline among reeds. For the rhythm of water would be the turbulence of the rhythm of air, and the rhythm of the earth would be the turbulence of the rhythm of water. And the theorem of the garden would be the door to the grotto.

"Perhaps on the other hand it isn't the souls that reincarnate in things but things which are reanimated in souls." Engraved on a monolith. Quixote does not stop. Sensing a strong suction toward the exterior in his left ear. The ground having warped as if it were a bridge.

And on reaching the place where the martin grimaces, he won't see the carp's scaled forehead, but the bubble weighted down at the bottom by buckshot.

And Quixote interpreted that it is not the appearance of things that hides the souls, but that through their metaphysical peripheries the things appear. "Something like wicks and flames," he would say. The leap, or rather belly flop, of the toad midwife on the water's surface.

With what dragon-like grace will the library turn to the jade pavilion when Quixote spots it. And the dull movement of the rocks will continue slinking in feline ambush beyond the library to the recitation gallery. While the tops of every orange tree look like a turtle before the walls of the Buddhist temple.

Perhaps, on the other hand, the folds sustain as much as they adorn.

Neither antimonial, the hibernal city nor the aestival countryside, in the garden.

The permanent sensation of ludic espionage, that another thought, parallel, analyzes the focused positions, considered by one. The mystery of the lotus's dry and empty carpel, atop the stem that is dry and full and serpentine, the garden's baton, creaking, murmuring, singing. There expectation is spectacle. Every image there thin, not because of transparency but circumflexion. And no unroofing can stand in for that place. Neither of mansion, nor of city.

The flower's domestic preference,

> "Resounding species of the enclosure"

The geophonist's Economo,

> "Natural brace of the inheritance"

The guest actors' ranch,

"Fabulous scraps of kindling," Quixote might reply.

How much it must have cost the rock its hardness, and the water its descent. How much it must have cost the tree its pivot, and the wind its coiled spiral. How much their bodies must have cost the laws of mechanics, how much strength must have cost the strong, and inertia the inert. So much effort, and such a chore. How axilly the thing goes about unfolding, threatened, always, by reduction, by the script of its identity. It costs, how much and how, to unfold itself in contrast toward the three or four essential words, pure antonyms, nuclear in the unfoldings, more and more, of the thing, of the bodies of the law, of the legal bodies, of the most transient transgressions that are more and more transient, and perhaps nucleated by the three or four wordless essences, pure annihilators, pure fuses, vaginal. "Wordless and yet pure conversant, pure sheather, purifying.

"Tests with no shortcut, fugitives with no subterfuge or skips because every single one of their nuclei have vaginal cores.

"Where has so much war been seen and so much respect in war. Where has so large an assault been seen and so much caution in the assault.

"That such circumspection should be so fitting, if not in the garden.

"Let rhythm be the inertia of the air in the water, and let rhythm be the inertia of the water in the earth, let the force of fire in the earth be rhythm, and let the force of the earth in the water be rhythm" Quixote would feel hearing "how the rhythm of the fire would move from inside the flesh to outside, from inside to outside the inert earth of water, inert water of air."

"Through another rhythm, that of the hook, the grapple, the pulley, the siphon, that of the force of earth in water? And what would that have to do with love? What would that have to do with the garden?" Quixote would ask, and "through the force of terrarum inauditarum, of the anchor line's Archimedean and tidal depths, consecrata, fortia fallitora.

Voice-carrying rhythm, force of earth in water, the garden's dramatic deposit. For the seasons wouldn't have fallen from heaven, but would climb, climb up themselves, penetrating themselves preocularly, perpetually and capillarily shearing themselves. Beware the garden.

> The omnicreasing inertia of air
> The shaping inertia of water
> The presenting force of fire
> The besieging force of earth

and though Quixote doesn't reply he would go about imagining the memory of the climacteric, Junoesque nocturnal tree. The theorem tree at the gate to the grotto, on the east side of the garden, and the semidouble soul suspended between two branches, collected in the night of the night tree.

"And even so the caged life, Nature on the wall, like caged life the poem in meter, caged life, like the canvas in the frame, the statue on the pedestal, the house under the eaves," Quixote would repeat. "For Antigone leaves no doubt that Oedipus's behavior wouldn't have been that of a settler of art but a settler of reinduction, and he would not have founded a city of liberty, but a city of vindication, and that the exostosis, in the form of a leaf, on the outer edge of his foot distracted the Sphinx from the full-footed index, violating untamed Nature's duties ad portas, causing the emergence, not eruptive, of the mausoleum of air, its pillars crowned with stylite oaks and hackberry and maples and seated on lichens and salty mosses." He would see, through the other garden door, decadent Luoyang, in the mottled green of dawn, and even in its still arrogant abrasive air, even in the immensity of its still precipitous natural moment, not in the remaining dirty lather, the chimerizing and beslimed foaming, but in the world's denighted raiment, this is all the world, the skinned raiment of the alba dolens, wrinkled and whipcracked by the forces of evil from one side, by the forces of metaphysics from the other side, and in the metalloid light of alba dolens he would see the sails blanketed, but it was not the world's ghost ship what would advance toward the zenith, not the psychophorous archangel on its wavy flight that he would see advancing, but a word, cursive, all the forces of evil on one side, pounding and parrying the minimal resistance like a battering ram. All the forces of metaphysics on the other side, pounding and parrying the maximum resistance like a piston, the maximum resistance of the raiment. And all this would constantly mark the raiment, constant mark on the illusion of a varied wrinkling always, varied and unrepeatable. Every sunrise.

"And on that raiment, works of art?" Quixote would exclaim to himself. He would be about to answer with more questions, when the blind woman creates a relief in the hollow.

She will have her left hand lifted to the height of her face, and her palm will explore the vertical plane before her toes.

Her right hand will be laid on the back of the left to gauge the pressure. Her steps will have been high-kneed. At no time will she have bent her neck.

The rooster will crow beneath the pomegranate tree.

The forces of evil gridlining the robe to count it, categorizing the account to cage it.

Only beneath pomegranates does the rooster crow.

Robing the pain on the other side, the robe paining and pleasuring itself.

And the blind woman wrapped in a patchwork quilt.

Wrinkling and parrying, caging, this is how evil would participate, complicitly, in the grand design, stamped on the robe.

And the blind woman nestled, transmersed, hieratically, on the threshold.

Putting bodies in the areoles.

But, the violence, eh, the violence of the metaphysical forces on the robe, formidable in art, terrible in pleasure? violence, of the metaphysical forces on the robe, in its rhythms? even in that of fire, rhythm of the white falcon, the rhythm of Avalokiteshvara?

Quixote would have come to the blind woman's left hand. Under his tunic the blind woman's tempted hand and tempting hand will explore Quixote's chest, underarms, belly, and thighs, and her lips will lay a kiss there where Quixote could

have had, will have had present, would have presented supernumerary breasts.

Coming to the vertical plane before the toes of the blind
woman, whose left hand under Quixote's tunic will precede
the supernumerary flesh-toned kisses on his conjectural nipples. On his maximum conjectural nipples.

"And the peony bud, what fold shall it be in this autumn
night?" it will matter little that it has been said and has been
thought and it won't matter at all who has said or thought
it, whether Quixote, the blind woman, or a third party, when
the raiment is tucked away in its absence of interlining.

When the pelican angel plummets or where the pelican
angel plummets. Through the crack of hyperbolic margins
infinitesimally close to the conical vertex. But coincident
only an infinite degree. Where only the horse sees centaurs.

But infinitesimal only symmetrically.

Maximal angels striving to breach the rhonchus chasm of
a word ambushed in the case where only the monkey hears
the delivery.

The blind woman's fold, coincident fold, fold at the edge,
fold between two eyelets, the comedic fold, and behind the
bottom of the end the origin's fold, the blind woman's fold,
tragicomic fold.

Maximal words striving to breach an angel.

Where only the monkey hears:

supositi merarias aus nités axim tuplame and other rubble.

ateuz

chc

x

h

"Infinite the mouth of the profile
Infinite the eye of the profile
Infinite the nose of the profile.
Infinite profile of the smiles
And infinite profile of the cries.
Auricular fullness of the profile
Auricular perfection of the profile
Auricular finiteness of the profile.
The savior sex of the spirits.
And the infinite profile of laughter?" Quixote will whisper, one temple supported by the blind woman's clavicular hollow, among thuribles of musk, sperm, and cyprine, among wavering lips and depilated tongues, in the mid-sensation of swallowing the beloved's eyes and of having one's own eyes sucked by one's brain, the very occupation center of the locus sui, collusive domination of the locum tenens.

"Easy for you to lose space, but impossible for a woman," the blind woman will say, "since the effect of our virtuality, our comedy, the virtuality of our comedic fold, has never been lost," including herself in Luoyang's vacuolation of the second plane, "for our virtue will always precede every tragedy, even every smile, and even every" Luoyang like the fraying of her profile "success" and the night, like a gargoyle staring at its lap, would be reclining on Luoyang's highest cornice in "only innocent of regeneration," due to the change in pitch including the round in the blacksmith's district "to each exodus only guilty of founding only innocent of foundation."

While Luoyang appears in the center of the blind woman's opening, the garden works would leave margins on either side of Quixote, making him the nuclear margin of a space whose vanishing point would turn, rotating in both directions, a tangent escape to everything. Like a ray of cinematographic projection in search of an infinitely distant screen, Quixote's words will trace on the blind woman: "trembling plasticity of the infissionable world, medusean tremor, such sublime plastic that at no point can an underlying rhythm be enthused without doing wrong at another, subtle plasticity that at every point of the universe brings near its possibility of pruning again with its possibility of perfection, malleable guide of the mysterious authority of the state of affairs, of the bridge woman, urbanizing plurality of woman, guide responsible for fossil regressions, precipitous molder, mystery of the chasms, infissionable which metaphysical plea does not control, metainfissionable only, impenetrable woman. Disturbing and anemophilous plasticity, how could one not understand this town's mystic suicides, pierce yourself and reside in the rhythms, that no man's land between the infissionable world and the metainfissionable, not to pierce yourself but base oneself where you don't temporize and to be the rhythms in which time resides, how could one not understand its refined lovers, attract you and accommodate the rhythms, culminating them where the instant bursts, not bursts but turns, not turns but axles, how could one not understand its patient eroticism, protractedly and repeatedly engaging your qualities, engaging all your bracing qualities, how not to understand the hangover of power brothels emit, the violence the gynaeceum emanates, the inherent evil in your urban exaggeration, in your hyperbolism in the city, by mere iteration of the intensive, by mere ultimation of the extensive."

Neither will Quixote see the neckless monkey dancing a chaconne in the garden sand, erasing the rake lines. Nor the shadow of the horse sticking out an eight-inch tongue and making as if to squeeze in. Nor the suggestive similarity between human soles and faces, between both soles and the semblance. Nor the irreflexive one between the backs of the hands and the encephalon. Nor flying with two elm leaves to the swallow. Nor avenging with two open eyes to the boy.

Who wouldn't swear that the Luo River had stopped and its filmy, tattered soul skirted the greenfinch cliffs leaving on their blunt teeth the tattered rags of a serpentine shirt. The sky sucked by its twists the clouds by its condensations by the light alcoholized by the earth. And trimmed in dazzling white, a descending blue stain on a horizon at Luoyang's nadir would form pools.

The strands of the blind woman's hair coiling their whole length one on top of the other until uncovering a slight capillary discoloration. Quixote would start to count the grays, but would quickly only observe them, amazed.

Behind the blind woman's profile, behind the city, the pale yellow sky will hold a wicked bunch of men in confrontation, above the eroding of the River Li, where parts of the angel will appear, the right knee, for instance, ashen, the corner of a great wing, ashen too, the left stump, lighter, but no fingertip, all caught among the loose rocks, thus, under the men stuffed with adipocire, hanging from the rigid sky.

And the remoteness of the western profile, beyond the city's great market, will the lure the impossible inversion of the double beloved, the hippanthropic inversion, all the subjected souls, aborted satellites, in a single black tulle.

But the last of its nest homunculi will be harmonious and will have his arms raised, aimed at the center of the inversion.

"Your drives would have remained, the negative violence of your access in me, embraced by vanity, return, and fullness, by overflow, haste, and faintness, by incontinence, empire, and overstep, sheathed, and thus amplified.

"From one woman to another, the same phallic servitude, the same ordered, violent, and gynophilic art, the constant religiosity of your styles."

"But where do you know me from?" and from the corner of his mouth a drop of saliva will lodge at the bottom of the blind woman's claviculed quarter-round molding.

"Not yet. I would just recognize you."

"And I long for you," Quixote will noisily slurp his already abundant saliva and feel the chill of the air on his teeth.

The transparent angel of sloth, the lazy angel of the rounds, feet in the sky, his shadow paddling on earth, cherubic marker of circumedenic cities, will pass through the blind woman's back.

"Why would you have refracted me in your narcissism?" she will ask Quixote. "Why wouldn't you renounce the part entirely and exclusively mine in you?" she will remind him.

"Oh, don't start again, and especially not pretending to want to finish."

"Apply the tale to yourself."

Other cherubs will come join forces with that one, some accompanied by celestial dogs and some by dwarves armed like Hoplites, creating certain confusion but without letting themselves get distracted. Nor by the radiant conicity, the radiating conicity of the world of confinement.

And from there it will be intelligible to them that the civil foundation will have been owed more to the origin's error than the course of the end.

On this side, Quixote's rhythm of air will be better articulated with the blind woman's rhythm of water than with his own, but both of their terrestrial and igneous rhythms will have turned to their dorsal seclusions.

And Quixote will feel that his legs will be born from two women facing the same side, and that his strabismic face, convergent in the eyes and divergent everywhere else, will be born from his own legs. From the same side toward a harlequinesque cherub.

The lubricious sky dogs.

"I will give a land to the fire and I will give a womb to the earth

"And the water and the air will shape a face," the anonymous one will have said.

"That which is less grave you all will call superior
Mistaking continents and contents
I will give a mirror to your understanding
And you will only know how to choose ambivalence
I will show a game to your reality
But you will only know how to represent importance
In summer the air will drink in the heat
And the rostrate womb will channel the waters," the
anonymous one will have said.

"Who would strangle with the knot of history, leaving the ruins of art at the city gates?" he will whisper in the blind woman's ear.

"Puber pu puberty puber puberty," she will answer Quixote.

"From an ear of foam Venus is born, arriving at the Nile Delta, Persian Gulf, the Indus Delta, the yellow gulf, engendering the throbbing shore of her profile, mixing the rhythm of fire and the rhythm of earth, engendering the sharpening edge, the voluntary edge" and as the tip of Quixote's tongue firmly traces the blind woman's auricular helix, he will see beyond the chrysanthemum-lined avenue of the Bronze Camel and its towered gate, beyond the Imperial College, the first signs of liveliness around the Foreigners Inn, heading toward the market at the Bridge of Eternity.

"With what preconceived bad faith, leave me! as if we didn't have more responsibilities, much more than to preserve, than your ends, than our ends, than our mission, against the preemptive attack of your committing, against your aggression, and that such preservation, temporary, won't need administering and defense, savings and measure, while you circle like tigers around all that grows, while you ambush the cities, inhabiting them illegally wilded, to prey more treacherously, under that color, upon the pretexted ruins, as if we women didn't have the deposit of the original answer, moreover, the deposit of the original alternative."

"To live or to die."

"No. To live or be born."

Apsara and dragon, tangled by their fraying tails, will go to roost on the blind woman's temple, while the speckled doe and the mounted hunter detach from her lambdoid hair, gaining breath, and the blind woman's earlobe is caught between Quixote's canines.

"Even this Buddhist city is a colony of Juno Moneta, and all the precaution of its sacred will comes from that mother."

"Would you return to the charge, telling the city to go to the countryside with weapons for products, and the countryside to the city with products for money?"

"No, so long as the weak take revenge in advance, the children among them, the women among themselves, abstracting precaution."

"And what does it abstract, enigmatize, the slogan you coin: May work be the trophy of leisure. That is why you only beautify us alone."

"That the muses have called the memory money, that precaution would abstract, that enigma would coin, only that would exclude your beauty."

"That the city be a mint of artworks, and art, the borough of a mint, and that you men have called it so, would exclude for us our beauty."

The monkey will whisper to Quixote:

> From the south seas
> A guest arrived
> And only delivered to me
> A mermaid's tear,
> And in that pearl
> There were nebulous signs,
> What was locked in its lines
> Did I procure to remove.
> Wrapped I put it
> Inside a small box
> So as to be able to pay
> The imperial tax.
> Blood it had become
> When I opened it again:
> What will become of me today,
> I have nothing else!

And the blind woman the prompter:

Squealing of carts, horses that whinny!
Each prince with a bow and quiver at his waist;
Old people, children, and women run alongside
And the dust conceals from them the bridge over
                                        the river.
So then we know it already: it is not good, having
                                        children
And a daughter will always, always be worth more
For we will promise her to our good neighbor
While the son lies unburied on the steppe!
How well you paint, general, you are inspired:
You paint the men of value with truth.
But on fixing your attention
Between lances and shields
Upon those who are at the roadside
It is you who bears the sideways looks!

and an acorn will bray.

Quixote will press his ear close to the blind woman's.

"Yes. Death between life and love," Quixote will say.

"Art between life and death," the blind woman will echo.

"Survival between life and art," Quixote again.

"Every pubescent would be wedged between childhood and woman," the blind woman will say.

"Every girl child will be first born," Quixote will echo.

"All art would affiliate the auspices training the thumb," the blind woman again.

Cold gusts clipped by the Mangshan mountains and re-gurgitated by the high Han Wall would lap Quixote's nape and the blind woman's profile before he sees them in the lighting torches of the fifteen imperial residences and their flicker in the ponds, before they are braided in the needle-like flickering of Bear's Ear Mountain.

Never would the dawn have risen so at length in the sky to give time to the first step and the first grasp, give time to the time of ordinally void consciousness.

Hereafter, overcoming the obstacle of iridescence and surface, path to perfection, namely, that to decontaminate art contributes to the dilution of identity, decontamination of death and survival, diluting the folds in the rhythms, rhythms in love, love venturing contributes the alien perfection, what is perfected only venture, perfect only what dilutes, not presenting the revision in the representation of the past. Not the triple face of death but the mixed double and periodic half. Not the sacred journey of legal measure but the distant faciotalar variation. Not the mesh of alimonial affiliation but the counter-mesh of every lover crucified by the beloved. Not the infinite sideways love. The hemless transfinite. The determined opposition

The ear's fetality. The single-yolked asymmetrical halves. The aural abduction of the earth. Binaural, rather. The pendency of waiting. All waiting. And may the city explain our sensory pettiness.

The rationing of vengeance. The salaried revindication of a bureaucratic forgetting. The imposture of the trunk invested with importance.

The antitragic arrogance of the warning. The anticomedic pusillanimity of the threat.

The fatigue of the rhythm of the air. Of its spaciousness. The plantation of the rhythm of the earth having planted the rhythm of the water. The protopolitan Cain. Hemipyric.

The agrarian origin of the civilized art. Its resident condition. Its invincibility, its famous possibility.

The virgin farmer and the whore farmer. The agrarian institutions of woman. The division of fire.

Agrarian the urban crises and agricultural all of its revolutions.

The lanes of stumps, the lines of facades, rows of soldiers, economic, political, military quartering. Quartering administration of space, quartered history. The sleeping quarters of the original spoils.

Quixote and the blind woman in the cramped space of the threshold, beneath the lintel of the garden. Feet sheltered in their square. The sun does not intercede with the clouds but yellowishly defines their crests. The pagodas, the towers, hunker. May all Luoyang's smokes spin horizontally. And the muted archeology.

That day, the night will resist the siege in the garden, and the dawn will last on the threshold. "Why, at the bottom of the path eager for love, when its acquisition would be renounced, and that renunciation would be offered, and that offer would be gratified, must they arise, from the woman's background, translucent, through the beloved's fold, opercularly through her second fold, the ancestral and descendant lasso, demanding, what, there, why, the ancestral lasso and the descendant lasso? what, relative to violent death, why there? why violent?"

"A frenzied avulsion, is that how it would be? distressing, while the man, who, having entrusted all narcissism to his twin, will renounce more than he will offer, and will gratify less than his offer, and will not have been able to delegate to his twin all the surveillance of his image, of the religiosity of his genital deposit," the blind woman will reply.

"Don't stop! How, and without that surveillance, abandoned in the pure dream of love, the dream without fantasy."

"Don't stop!"

"It would be enough, if that's all it consisted of, it would be simple, too simple."

"If it consisted of a single fold being enough for a woman, it would be incredibly simple, and that woman, very simple."

"Damn you," Quixote will mutter.

But the crags of both ears will coat the whisper in metal.

"For you, yes. The claimants won't have asked you to explain me, but to understand me."

"That deluge of history in the depths of love. How to understand it in you! In a work of art, sure. But in you. And that it should be introduced artistically. Sculpturally even. Artistically but not ruinously. New, not ruined. As if freshly-made. In the very violence of its novelty, of its health. More than a deluge of history, a deluge of animalized art. Why will it so demand—mortally, violently—the history of its form? That? Why will they demand the history of their forms in the depths of an embrace? The most unnatural violence, to demand, after dying, before being born."

"Wait! I feel none of that!"

"Because you are complicit!"

Quixote will hear the blind woman swallowing spit as if it were his own, "and the more woman you are, the more complicit you will be in that claim, artistically, lovingly! How can you not feel its direction? All violence, in which direction would it not go? And don't tell me: don't look!" The blind woman will peel away her ear from Quixote. On her black screen he will see the world's cross, history cut into its two threads, the infinite string of kinship crossed by the infinite string of lovers. In the woman's profile, he will see the reflection of the man cutting the thread of blood. He will see the georgic cone in the sky and the earth's orb attacked by harmony, loaded like a bullet with an urban ramrod. And artistic gunpowder. He will see the spouses always with their backs turned on their witnesses. He will see the son holding the stool and the stirrup. And among tents, he will see the monkey's bulging eyes.

As for Quixote, his eyes will follow the blind woman as she leaves the cramped space, but at the precise moment she finishes turning halfway around once outside, he will see what he will have seen. Nothing else.

On the woman's belly, three rhythms and two folds, incompressible, informative, cerebral, pyrotaphic, only natural thing without adversity, only natural thing with eschatology, hinge under a bottle at sea, under a salted and sunned shell, three rhythms and two folds, flower like the flower's fruit, fruit like the fruit's flower, improjectile, insubmissable, the dress's ark, and the decorative edging of all dresses, sieve of summer, water's informary, heap of mirrors, repeater of tropes, cheek of horse herd, bubbling over river stones, commotion over the serenade and place over the truth, shirt of god, sleeve of sentry, shape of the soul and vehicle for the foot, speed of conics, flight of topsails tipped toward the sky, Janus's fish traps, dream in contempt, blinking without simultaneous eyes, story with no titles, and word with no stories: do not say, lovers, that you have undressed on the bed and undone even the canvas aged by you and wrinkled on the inert ground, for into the most complex fold will go the simplest and in yours the pleating of the globe will find center do not believe for the orphaned aftermath of love that in an ambimanant halo you have limited and protected yourselves for the sphere will go to the cone and in yours the curved branch of death will find center under survival and then under the life enveloping survival but separating survival from life alone do not call yourselves immortal nor believe yourselves invisible for the simplest death will go to the most complex death and in yours the second fold of survival will find center for the simplest rhythm will go to the most complex rhythm and in yours the consonance of life the comedy of life the ensemble of life will find center: wholeness in you that completes itself, the same day of the same night, framework of occluded folds of historical space, and compress of its ulcerated perforating depths from the same position on the very side, beating of the blue, bleached tree, three rhythms and two folds, head support on the tooth by the body on the nail, genitor born of the life of its offspring, genitor reborn from the death of its offspring, alive indeed born from the dead self, earth's radiated primacy over the hanging deflections, angel of the gorget, ridge of consciousness, on the woman's belly, Quixote's red head.

Lively the blind woman leaves Quixote back turned to the garden and blindly fans the marble balustrades and plinth dragons down the avenue from the pavilion that imposingly guards with grilles the altar of a temple twice roofed and once crowned, blindly skewers the steps for men's knees between landings for cart axles up the avenue from pavilions saddled with adornments to uniform the entrances and exits, feels her way along trapezoidal doors wider at the lintel than the threshold like hollow keystones of anything that isn't ground, briefly haloing the vertexless angle of the passageway, feeling the tower arch with a fertile stolon down the avenue from a turret that shows, by both lights, the tree-like roof decorated with bird-stabbing spikes, tapping her cane on long-legged pontifications of waves spiraled by carding tigers up the avenue from the palace undetected by the guards on the, rounds the corner shocked by the crash of overhangs and, like a thrice-tiered sharp chamfered edge one for the avenue to gauge from the interlocked traffic below between the screen walls before doors decorated with flying horses, feels the portico in its political and religious constitution up to its prominent chamber and recessed prestige, feels the suspending waters of the small marble columns that branch flower and flame toward the horned and bearded horses after over without, according to the belvedere, two elephants, bundles of caution handfuls of decorative shelving for brackets on the plinth with the halo fallen to the hem, down the avenue from the base of prayer wheels staggered between dovetail bells, blindly prunes the stupas of the lotus that floats in the mother-of-pearl cup that would sink cylindrically through its bulging collector still toward the avenue below with the sunshades of the embrasures in a gigantic ruffled row of bulwarks, feeling the rampart between the fields and the grass or the sandal and the horseshoe or the crossbow and the bow between the sun-dried and the tanned or the coin and the trade or the stool and the stirrup rampart between air and wind or canal and creek or census and cycle between possession and usufruct or key and buckle or silo and spoke the rampart between the domestic arts and the arbitrary arts or in well-founded power and sliding power or the hierarchical childhood or untamed widowhood between the courtyard of statues and the market of anecdotes or the roads administration of laborers and the amusement of comrades or the recruitment of whoremongers and the desire of volunteers feeling the rampart between the shooting man and the sprinting man or between the man of straight lines and the man of curves or between the stationary man and the punctual man or between the man on credit and the man in person or between the occupying man and the driving man or between the rarifying man and the epidemic man or between the echoing man and the man of one time only or between the discovered man and the man of another man's one time or between the consumable man and the transferential man or between the surrendered man and the unmissable man or between the intestate man and the democratic man or between the retractable man and the man without his one thing for each thing or between the forbidden man and the urgent man or between the stringing man and the man at loose ends or between the awarding man and the stamping man or between the exploiting man and the man between right eyes or between the man for every alibi and the man for every confrontation and at the end of the rampart she will spit on the ground and feel the gentle grasses and feel the fierce grass until the square, indigo grain that guides the desert sands.

The revisited man will reenter the garden. Beside him a granite boulder will roll along the ground marked by the parabolic descent of instruments with no further denominating usage for a job begun and no longer beginning. On the horizon, the sun will become polar casting rods of light for support toward the skies and the lands to fix itself becoming more ray than globe while a backlit black apsara will sustain a lunar rainbow over the cranes in the pond.

Along the ground marked by the parabolic descent of instruments. He will reach the condemned pavilion from whose fortress chiseling sounds will reach him.

Reamer track that files sawing that cuts measuring that will denude opening bottles that will unscrew opening cans that bolts opening the lids of words, back screwed for being too bearing. He will reach the wall coffered with basal numeral natural novenas.

He will reach the temporal corner of dimensional space where the mannish and crossed-dressed angel will remain, assisting with wings the prime woman's midday.

From the trodden fold or the fucked fold would hang a disc, loupe on one side and mirror on the other, whether imprinted or unknown.

Through the loupe, he will see reflected the polyhedral time of the serpentine hypocephalus. Through the mirror, he will see the inverted image of the other childlike angel carving a little hand from jasper.

The ladder lowered from the sky will not reach the earth. He will not know that two men are worth more than their languages nor will he say that the languages of man and woman are worth what they are. Intrigued and perplexed he will look at the ladder twisting the sky like a stiff pennant.

He will wish to enter in the loupe's reflection but he would encounter a horse's head with crustaceous eyes raised over a neck on which the body of the monkey asleep on its side has been tightly incorporated, as he would simultaneously wish to enter the mirror's inversion but for the fact that the little hand, reversed and colossal, would come out to meet him.

Colossal until it comes close and makes him feel the stinging ice of melancholy in the failed replacement's internal aura.

The aura of the failed replacement confined in the jasper like the rhythm of fire in the rhythm in the rhythm of the motionless stone.

Motionless it will suddenly reemerge oriented to the west where solomonically the eye of God and the eye of Satan will seal the sky.

VIII

LULLABY SANS BEMOLS

The visitor makes peace
Between the father that would have signed
And the corner piece
That does not occupy the fourth corner,
The mother who only
Renounces herself
And the son who abandons
His voice and the prophet
Who fears his ability,
He who survives future fame
And the daughter
Who dies for fame past.
For the echo diminishes
When the baby has survived
Or the bachelor has propagated,
When the young man will have known
That the lass will meet him,

And the when the young woman
Complemented what the woman
Retracts.
That possibilities are desires,
Condition is the order,
And the qualities that modify
The infinite
Are names.

One, two, but, the third step, raised over one of its extremes. In front of him, a beam, like the body perfectly cylindrical and matte black of a thick headless and tailless serpent, in That erect floating, rolling around its axis. The two steps, and both levels of the desert, covered in glassy varnish, melted and frozen sand, with marks of currents at odds with one another. Before reaching the horizon, an abyss, such that he will have to descend to the mountains to be able to climb to its valleys, surrounding the desert. With the stars in radials, permanently in night, a crown of sky, at the zenith of the abyss. Beyond the horizon and cut off by it, the heads of stiff-necked steeds. Between the step and the beam Hydattila will have arrived, carrying the exotic branch of a deciduous tree:

"Have I felt excessively in myself the defect of another body? another person's defect in my person, in my alienation for the sake of gaining an identity, the alienation of another for the sake of losing an identity? have I felt in my desire another's hate? in my first possibility of death his last impossibility of living? or in my panic the sudden consolidation of his unreality?"

On the other side of the step, seated on the ground, Sheba, Bad Whore and Good Whore, and Antigone chat idly.

"...unless the most attractive thing for a woman is a man's mind..."

"No way! His full purse, and I'll loosen it up for him..."

"Even if he has to tighten his belt after that?"

"Sure, so I can loosen it right up again."

"Haha...haha..."

"Don't tell me that in a man, the outline of his thighs, strong, in his clothing, doesn't make you..."

"That his strengths make his destiny ... cooperate with the hero ... graft onto his greatness of spirit ..."

"... what he knows and thinks, nothing as much as everything ..."

Emerging from the abyss, he laid one hand on the edge of the desert, then the other. Quixote's head followed, and his body, supporting itself at the waist a while before rolling onto one hip and standing. Quickstep, he came toward Hydattila in a rush:

"In this, hope was the form habeas corpus took to appear with caution and thus hand itself over to its precedence, even if the initiation journey in the exoteric review of every stop that published the women to words without connotation failed, even if the white is fleeting. What were you saying? how feminine the blackbird, the woman with complete freedom, free, even, from one's own stage in life, free from the imprint of that stage on another person, and even when the rivalry of one's double meant only that the awareness of their sex was incomplete in both ..." On reaching Hydattila he grasped his branch with both hands, between which he let his panting head hang, and in time heard him say:

"Counterpacing their love, the lovers must have traded karmas."

He fell to his knees, and then cottoned on to the eloquent:

". . . the woman who eats and drinks in the shelter of a man . . ."

". . . the one who arranges the victories on her two branches . . ."

". . . the one who knows how to carry on her camouflage and not repeat it."

Moved by the hyaline glints, Hydattila will have seen on the ground his face, inverted face and with closed eyes. He will have raised the eyes that Quixote opened, seeing in the step's smoothness a countenance that ceaselessly regenerated its contents before their approaches to wholeness and in this way successively overflowing their contours in such a way from a profile, including the segments of the contour between the contents of the countenance like fires in an oval's opal, appearing in such a way to rotate the silhouette from every perspective for each perspective around an axis of a symmetry always avoided and stolen from the evidence so that it gives dandadrjskgfxnzzzrrrrrrr quadrilateral folds of closure of a revoked glance.

". . . from the garrison of the origin to the garrison of the end, may the woman unfold the fan of her wisdom . . ."

". . . may it reach from her thighs and her belly to her kidneys and her nape . . ."

". . . from when her birth crosses a man's death until her death crosses that man's birth . . ."

Quixote lifted one knee, on which he leaned to stand up, not releasing the other hand from the branch, and joined the conversation:

"I knew a woman who was on her way to that, from all that . . ."

Hydattila might have debated this, but turning to the women:

"Have I found a woman on her way to that, toward all that . . ."

Pressed against the edge of the step, Thalia's arm is a brace for her body, which turns almost halfway toward Hydattila and Quixote. At her temples and on both sides of her nape, she wears a diadem of cranberry twigs. Her chin is as clear as her forehead, and her cheekbones match her lower eyelids just as well as her upper lids match her nose. Her mouth resembles a fawn on a cushion:

> "You were in popular art
> And you might have been in highbrow art
> When you passed through the capital
> With your ration of individual law
> You might have passed where the dovecote
> Pardons between the oasis and the garden.
> You were in historical business,
> You might have been in unequaled leisure,
> When you walked to morning worship
> You might have walked where the evening exults

From crepuscular philosophy.
You were in exemplary love,
And you might have been in final love,
When you loved manifoldly
You might have loved where the mind is double."

The heads of all steeds turn around the horizon, right to left. Seated on the beam, chin in hand and elbow on knee, were four archangels, the transpositor, the andromachus, the antemophore, and the mute one with mussed wings and no portfolio. But it was the Specter of Absalom who spoke out, emerging from of the beam like a genie from a lamp:

"Oh! defiled sister!"

Pressed against the other edge of the step, Ipsibidimidiata's arm is a brace for her body as she turns, showing three of her half-profiles:

"From forced love the soul's tar is made, its blackest and thickest pitch, the bitumen of its rainboots, the tar of its stored memories, and why do you bring them into the light?"

"So that you do not become an invocation."

Quixote releases the branch and without turning halfway around admonishes:

"And torment whom? what was the fetishistic behavior?" he opens his hands, palms forward, and takes one step toward Ipsibidimidiata:

"You wouldn't let yourself be lost, and I needed to lose you to increase my love, and as was logical, I went back to the point of origin so as to lose you ever farther behind. I remembered our duet poems, and our vows of perfection in a pantographic world of Rome. And from those trips, the onirism of a desire, patient and spiteful, gradually built up, until I lived almost completely asleep, and only a bit in the vigil of poems begun without answers . . ."

Ipsibidimidiata folded her hands:

"And I played along, waiting for you in the oblivion of what I could still know of you, and in the ignorance that my works contained your inducements, and even, perhaps mainly, when they were in opposition to the incentives of your inducements, in the vagueness and apathy of our mutual assumptions, of our growing lack of reciprocal initiative, separating us under the convention of our endeavors and commitments, drifting apart without dismantling it, and leaving our tokens like enchanted scarecrows to promise an incredible return . . ."

Melantho and Living Son of a Bitch emerge, pulling Dead Son of a Bitch by the hand, from the same point in the abyss through which Quixote appeared. Without pause, they say to Hydattila as they pass:

"Patience, with your duplication and what is halved by those who love."

Laocoön emerges behind, and with stiff, great strides, he comes to stand before Hydattila and behind Quixote:

"Where the worship of ancestors does not require art and where art transcends the apotheosis, there you will find Ipsibidimidiata composing the nonreferential, from the hidden side of the tombstone and the outer face of the dome until you two compose the enigma that has no representation and therefore no consequent difficulty, until you two compose the relative fold of all forms, through which the oldest thing is but an embryo, through which the peasant is no longer religious, where the citizen does not idolize his mortality, and where art shares a fold with Nature, there you find Ipsibidimidiata, there you find only Ipsibidimidiata and Attila finds only Thalia, in a parallel space, a different, simultaneous time, where never again when, where where doesn't happen, where nothing else happens, where he finds himself, there you find that the date has no deadline, there you find the square with no market, with no mercy, the peristyle with no architrave, the peristyle of flight, toward the horizon and toward the sky . . ."

Quixote was addressing Ipsibidimidiata:

"The alienation was the same, and yet in it, love had more reality. How was that?"

"Because then you forgot that the slave-groom songs inspired our poems."

The Specter of Absalom takes Ipsibidimidiata's words:

"Our poems for one voice, and in it, the fury of plural beauty . . ."

Quixote admonished him again:

"That voice was not Ipsibidimidiata's, and your poems inspired the people to familial sedition for historical revenge. It was you who was affected by our poems! Not us, nor the people's songs, for yours." The Specter of Absalom smiled, and the archangels winked.

Through the point at the edge of the desert diametrically opposed to Quixote's exit, Attila appears. His head, chest, and belly are uncovered, and the ridge of his nose, his sternum, and the linea alba reverberating. He heads toward Ipsibidimidiata, who, along with Quixote, was the first to sense him:

"He didn't precede us, then?"

"And still indicated our presence?"

Attila arrives. Silently, he and Ipsibidimidiata look into each other's eyes. Then:

"I am a desired woman, I was longed for, and I will have been ripened. I want to love. But like this. I am confused."

"It is still too early and it is too late. The present still does not tympanically resound. Desire is still too much for it. The hour of the flesh remains folded in love and in crime. Direction still makes sense in the place it isn't really. If, on one side, there is the concealing and concealed world, then on that same side there is necessarily the concealable and concealed world. Necessarily free. But the appearance that is not integrated drifts erratically through its aliquants. This is the difference between the individuality of origin and the individuation of the end. And in that difference, desire does not slacken."

Quixote drew breath to speak but first the Specter of Absalom:

"If it were easier to love without a body . . . In that case we could dispense with the origin and the end . . ."

But Attila:

"You dispense with the present, dispensing with the origin and the end. Listen, not only do you exalt yourself, but you do it poorly, well, in the worst way. The flight of the spirit doesn't change you any more than that of the body, and the more space you lose seeking shorter shortcuts, the shorter the drying time of perennialness. You are neither artificial nor natural, pure implication, neither complement nor supplement, but subcomplement. Just as art imitates Nature to take it out of religion, so you imitate fantasy to remove it from the dream, you are the imitation of the fantasy that wants to transcend its creation. But God . . ." and he turns his face to Quixote and his eyes to Hydattila, "who is the utopian capacity of the origin, and ceaselessly traverses creation, flapping toward the end it seems, what does he have to do with your abstraction of the present? Veiled by light, you imagine yourself uncovered, and uncovered by your imagination, you see yourself thoughtful and loving."

All those present before Attila look at his reverberating outline.

Quince-ripening light runs through the folds of the starless sky. Outside the Quixotic point, Solomon catches up to Laocoön. He carries with him a book, whose title *The Fruit of Life*, is freshly inked. Yet Laocoön gestures for it, and he hands it over. He addresses Attila:

"When there has been the whisper of the quadruple folds and Quixote has the unfortunate two-way task, it shall be justified and palpable that your responsibility aligns with his, without restriction or requirement to his good fortune and not according to where the weights may fall. And when state has its judgment in your opportunity, may his unrelated conscience not be the overturned receptacle of his associable soul where there's been no more sense than in the maximum form. Don't let him suffer more than that."

Laocoön turns over the book in his hand and addresses Attila:

"So long as there is no lesser meaning than in the maximum form. Don't make him suffer less than that."

Attila folds his hands over his belly:

"There is greater meaning than the maximum form just as there is lesser form than the minimum meaning. So, I only make him suffer what I permit him. For a body comes over his ethereal body to meet the intracorporeal body, to perform abandoning of sovereignty, comes to dethrone the empire of evil over pain, overthrow its usurpation, and restore conscience to its humility, its courage, its strength, in the pleasure of its strength, virtue, it comes to perform abandonments of sovereignty between bodies and between consciences, and not just between the evil of bodies and the pain of consciences, it comes to liberate form from judgment, to raise necessity, between providence and its rearview mirror, not just between the folds and between the halos, but also between the halo and the fold."

Attila makes a half turn and moves a few steps away. Quixote and Hydattila turn their backs on Solomon and Laocoön and they are heard mumbling:

"In the imperfection of my past, I hated the origin."

"In the perfection of my future, I will have loved the origin."

"In the imperfection of my past, I feared Nature."

"In the perfection of my future, I will have faced art."

"In the imperfection of my past, I loved Ipsibidimidiata."

"In the perfection of my future, I will have . . ." but Lao-coön interrupts him:

"Don't count your chickens . . . When your body falls in its consciousness, like pumice stone on a raft of oil . . . When all the rhythms of your body fall into the rhythm of its consciousness, and you know isolation without loneliness, company without communication, communion without presence. And then . . ."

"In my past, I was ignorant of inexpression," but Solomon interrupts him:

"Don't be content with what Attila tells you, for you still confuse inexpression and lack of communication, your senses are like dried beans in the roomy pod of your consciousness, tiny clappers of an immense bell, irreclaimable symbols in the allegory, lost identities in the imperceptible aura. That you still insist on symmetry, of the thought, and believe in the projecting perspective of the accomplished. You continue ignoring that there is so much light with no radius, light with no focus, in your past."

Quixote would like to address Hydattila but his memory originated in women's words, listened to or overhead, in women's names praised one after the other in his ear, in women's profiles loved immediately, silhouettes with no time for recognition, in faithful silhouettes hard to hold by the chin, retracting in the iterative splitting of the living mask, the memory of his consciousness originated, inserted between him addressing Hydattila, in the iterative portion of natural beauty, truth's partial petition, as always everything, between his attention while Hydattila will have mensurated the rhythm of his air with the rhythm of his water and mensurated the rhythm of his water with the rhythm of his earth, until emerging from its physicality, emerging from all possibility of language, his consciousness diffracting at its own limit, toward itself and from itself, until it makes the limit disappear, and its center as a result, all possibility of it, personifying, identifying, will have diffracted until altering nothing, until its continuity, purer than the consciousness of conic continuity.

Laocoön and Solomon lean toward Hydattila and Quixote:

"That through consciousness of its absence, space may be presented. That through consciousness of its temporal hypostasis, the present may be positioned, by the withdrawn consciousness of time, the subject may be indicated, as indicated as indicating, and can only be as protesting as another subject is protestable."

"Because the pain of the return is determined by the most faithful memory, but the love of that return, its quality, is determined by the falsest memory, you have to suffer more to not love less, finish recognizing to not start to forget, ending the word and the image, one with the other . . ."

The Specter of Absalom, forming a plume over Ipsibidimidiata's head:

"If I could kiss her aura, and thus merge with her innermost self more than a mortal could . . . and with her avenge the inadequacy of those who outlive me . . . if she were at least conscious of him now, and then I could . . . intermingle . . . frequenting her most concrete rhythm . . . frequent her in him . . . if only she . . ."

But Thalia:

"You kill survival by obeying the law, and you live death by obeying art, but my chosen daughter is conscious of an aura unfinished in a rosette, which you cannot contribute to completing with any section. The ruin of that aura haloes the ruins of other, less dense rhythms, in which the consciousness of repetition still prevails. What begins with the flesh ends with the flesh, and from a comedy that is performed, life comes away, total, detached from its smallest division, perfect life detaches from its own defect. This is why you cannot visit her most concrete rhythm, for you belong to the length of history, not its width, you belong to history for its folds of creation, not the folds of no return. In Nature's light background the political art of the classic floats. The wreckage of that art comprises the bucolic bosom of utopia. For dreams are also the origin's utopian fragmentation, and the mystery of the world agrees in that, the supernatural end of a natural origin. Hence your horror of emptiness, and the horror of dreams and classical art at emptiness. Hence the religion's horror at emptiness, and the horror of both the city and Nature at emptiness. Hence more than one person has the same dream."

Pressing a wing to his side, the contrapositor archangel lets himself fall like a whirligig. But again, the Specter of Absalom:

"And Quixote's horror."

Ipsibidimidiata looks up:

"Hence forgetting favors the anecdotal mass of global memory."

The Specter of Absalom sets his eyes on them:

"I wouldn't want to intervene out of fear."

Without turning, Attila answers him:

"It is not your difference from the body that frightens, but your coincidence with revenge. It is not your rhythmical problem, nor your withdrawal from the fold, but the unpresentability, the undilutability of your complaint. My affection for Ipsibidimidiata, her dear utopia and her beloved history, only offer you one perspective, only one and only indirect: not the corporative guild of the living artists, only history's artistic corps is possible for you. Find it."

"But, in Quixote . . . ?"

"Shush."

Quixote would like to address Hydattila but his memory originated in the consciousness of a woman gone senile for indefinitely repeating her youth, and he stammered the echoing roots of a proper name, regeneration of an image made senescent for overseeing its immanence, for surviving its imminence, roots spoken by an adolescent to her second in command, proper name made common for lack of communicable desinence, he stammered a radicality in progressive decomposition, differentiating without managing to transpose, serializing in an uninterrupted onomatopoeia, the solvable wrinkle of continuity in the image, a giant anagram that every adolescent wheezed in her second in command. Quixote would like to address Hydattila, but the consciousness of his pneumatic and hydraulic rhythm gave way to that of a retrogressive laughter, and not to the consciousness of his georgic rhythm, while Hydattila will have mounted the sacrum between his temporal pinnacles and blurted, wholly and without no tip whatsoever, the georgic rhythm with the consciousness of his pyrrhic rhythm, while he will have besmirched his chin and fingertips in the consciousness of his pyrrhic rhythm, and interwoven the full possibility of his consciousness between presence and identity, in the pyrrhic rhythm, the universal appearance, separating presence and identity, separating reflection and comparison, the gaping verse. Obvious.

Melantho and Living Son of Bitch return to the meeting between Quixote and Hydattila, pulling Dead Son of a Bitch:

"If art crucifies the present, the original exit from childhood crosses the specter's last entrance."

Art, how it will have taken him out of the city, how it will have passed him through the mother's treasured gates, how it will have led him to love, freeing him from the catarrh, freeing his temporal availability for the beloved, but Hydattila will have projected his pyrrhic rhythm onto the melancholy of deferred love, curdling the painful trail, embolizing the pyrrhic rhythm in that pain, intensifying the resulting consciousness, until it is perceived as sensitive, one like supreme conical density, he will have projected his pyrrhic rhythm onto the melancholy of deferred love through art and subsistence, through the very art that will have led him to that same thing which will have deferred for him, when he will have taken it out of the city, he will have passed it through the mother's treasured gates as Quixote brought out the most classical of all heroes, Heracles, from his titanic irregularity.

The archangel antemophore sighs, and a satin peony petal slips between cheek and hand.

Forehead to forehead, Laocoön and Solomon: "Don't think that ruins with structure can give Heracles political character."

And Attila turns, approaches Ipsibidimidiata and Quixote and Hydattila, and says to them in a low voice:

"Woman is the form of man because the present is the form of the future, when the future will have been the form of the past."

Ipsibidimidiata will have disappeared again when vanishing behind the edge of the step and Thalia's back, and Quixote walked away.

Laocoön pulls his forehead away from Solomon's and catches up to Quixote.

"Don't go back, what for? if your idea of the beginning is that of a progressive ingress and not that of an ingredient in the congress of the rhythms. Don't go back if your idea of art is that of making the city a garden and not that of including the order of the day in Nature. Don't go back, if your idea of woman is not the reform of her repetition that recaps her quantity."

Ipsibidimidiata, to the rhythm of her land, will have concentrated, from that sacral and tympanic sharpness, her consciousness within her solar rhythm, presentatively present, the folding between muqarnas, igneous, the work of the sun, igneously underlining all folds, hypophany and epiphany of the earth, and felt the melancholy of deferred love, stinging pain of the stinging consciousness of the stinging memory of the present, mother pain of pain, lamprey biting its own tail, leech inlaying its own belly, leeching rat of the soul. She will have projected, very calmly, her solar rhythm onto that pain, thus intensifying her consciousness, until feeling it, heavy as lead in the middle of her head, consciousness, neither solar nor painful, much more present than any other up till then, and much more georgic than the earth's beat, but pain overflowed, love differed, the flat value of survival leaned toward the distant verticality of life, consciousness in life thus discovering death in its own verticality, desiring it like a moment of life and for its immediate possibility, and Melantho and Living Son of a Bitch pulling Dead Son of a Bitch arrived in the divided consciousness she was suffering, suffering her backflowing consciousness in the beat of water and in the beat of air and Melantho and Living Son of a Bitch pulling Dead Son of a Bitch entered her as if entering their home, and Living Son of a Bitch observed her with the same seriousness that Melantho showed while contemplating Dead Son of a Bitch.

They will have breathed together, the aura and the tempest; they will have pulsed together, the drizzle and the torrent, each will have vibrated, the sand and the crag, each will have haloed, the firefly and the sun. Each will have thought, the pinch and the melancholy, they will have loved together in each one, neither double the half nor half of the double, Ipsibidimidiata and Hydattila, the omnipresent rhythm of the master fold, the promised diaspora of the works of art in Nature, the loosing of the constellations in the attic, to the head of the cones on the angels' mounting block, the conglobation of the pulps and the tongues, of the tongues and the eyes, the conglobation of the eyes and the brains, of the brain together in each of them, the invitation to set up house with growing stones on the stigma conceived by the concrete halo, the living life of the embodied flesh, the dead death of the spiritualized soul, the loved love of the figurative figure, entailed in each one without a plan for the crossing.

Quixote, to the beat of his water, would wish to live after history, would wish to love after melancholy, would wish to present the garden as an antiborough, but the pain overflowed, constraining its hydraulic beat toward the rhythm of the air, drawing him closer to death but distancing him from any other moment of life, and he desired suicide, if only to cease enduring, to put an end to the pain, and he remembered all the trees of the earth that Attila named for him in his childhood, the trees in bloom without their leaves, and he desired suicide, if only to not to animalize, not to vegetate, and his consciousness, alone in its rarefaction, isolated in its anguish, welcomed with the greatest sorrow the arrival of Melantho, and Living Son of a Bitch pulling Dead Son of a Bitch, and that Melantho was reciting his poems, Ipsibidimidiata's poems, and those they wrote together, which she carried in her hands.

Together breathed the aura and the tempest, together pulsed the drizzle and the torrent, together, Ipsibidimidiata and Quixote loved their daughter and their son, their girls and their boys, the string of their imagined progeny, the joy of being exclusive without being unique, the immanence of their conservation, innovating the renewable, discovering the restorable, the sea that dawned cloudy over the sand, the exhaling, lactescent dawn, dimming the adjacent while the stars gave off space, the rocking of the renown by increasing together, the throbbing rocking, the sighing dream, went out to meet a grand proletarian star.

One could shed their skin but could not change their shape because the skin would be inside the bone and the void would suck in the flaying frame for which all love's sorrow would be deserved, and when rationality would meddle in revenge and forgetfulness, the law would come to light, since there was nothing as politically historical as the imitation of Nature in its evacuation by a language-spooled lead line of the plundering of its deaf and sordid Uranian truth by the stowaway of history seeking the linear or silent limit between the real thing and the artistic thing and finding the rhythms and attempting the rhythm of the air to avenge forgetting by forgetting vengeance.

Antigone, Sheba, and Good Whore and Bad Whore rise in a curtain of water hung by the archangels and streaked by the sun, mimetic waters of that scene from the comedy in which the horsewoman quarrels with the flower seller's sighted guide, sustaining waters, female ephemerides, flower seller who carries a few eggs at the very bottom of a basket, sighted guide who never once looks back, horsewoman who cannot fight the woman, waters of a theater curtain that neither separates nor conceals though upon it the light generates a sound effect, upon it the horsewoman never engages the flower seller's sighted guide directly, only in the tangency of breach or bulge, and moreover the flower seller is always threatening to step away with each step, waters emptied of ballast, threatening to strew the flowers, decapitate them even, and dribble the eggs instead of leaving them to soak, risen from the varnished sand in the waters of a curtain up to the hyperboloid blue sky, on sounds sustained by fickle light and its ample absence, waters dressed in mourning, in artistic grief, sibylline swishing of body-less bulges.

Attila climbs two steps. He and Thalia holding hands:

"Finally we are born from our children in the majesty of day."

"Children who penetrate both twilights."

"We are born from our adoptive children."

"Free before our kin."

"We are beyond utopia."

"And because we are on this side of history." "We are in panoramic limbo." "Because we are present."

"By the light of day we see the creative effect of night."

"The most distant of powers in full effect."

"We see the cones' eggs."

"And the halo's shell."

"We hear the substitute's secret passion."

"And we touch the banister of spring running a hand over evening."

"Stumbling over the dead man we touch the duelist."

"And we hear the dance of eggs in every soul."

"We sense the wrinkling of celestial bodies."

"And the brush of the wrinkles."

"We feel the leap's contraction."

"And how distracted death is."

"We think the sense that calms the voice."

"The sense of grace."

"The monkey gesturing to the turkey on the branch smiles upon us."

"And we smile at the equestrian grandfather."

"We laugh inwardly at others."

"We laugh the outsides of the allusion."

ALIOCHA COLL (the pseudonym of Javier Coll Mata [1948-1990]) was a Spanish writer and translator raised in Barcelona who spent several years of his adult life in Paris, where he committed suicide after completing *Attila*. He is the subject of "Everything Bad Comes Back" by Javier Marías, and believed in *Finnegans Wake* as the "starting point" for contemporary literature. In addition to *Attila*, he wrote a couple novels, a play, and several essays, but the majority his work was either published posthumously or remains unpublished, despite Spanish super agent Carmen Balcells backing him throughout her life as the future of Spanish literature.

KATIE WHITTEMORE translates from the Spanish. Her translations include novels by Sara Mesa, Javier Serena, Aroa Moreno Durán, Lara Moreno, Nuria Labari, Katixa Agirre, Jon Bilbao, Juan Gómez Bárcena, Almudena Sánchez, Aliocha Coll, and Pilar Adón. She received an NEA Translation Fellowship in 2022 for Lara Moreno's *In Case We Lose Power*, and has been a finalist for the Spain-USA Foundation Translation Prize and the Queen Sofía Spanish Institute Translation Prize, longlisted for the Dublin Literary Award, and shortlisted for the National Translation Award.